MURDER IN MAASTRICHT

Master Mercurius Mysteries
Book Seven

Graham Brack

SAPERE
BOOKS

MURDER IN MAASTRICHT

Published by Sapere Books.

224 Trafalgar Road, Ilkley, LS29 8HH,
United Kingdom

saperebooks.com

ISBN: 978-0-85495-077-5

PROLOGUE

I am not a vain man [Manuscript note: my clerk, Van der Meer, just produced a disgusting noise from his nose which he claims was a stifled sneeze] but it is gratifying to note the public interest in my memoirs. Needless to say, I have presented the University library with a free copy of each successive volume, and occasionally I look to see how often they are being consulted, so I am delighted to say that it appears that no less than three volumes have been stolen by staff or students. Given that they would need to be able to read some quite long words I think we can rule out undergraduates as the likely culprits.

We have now come to the year of Our Lord 1686. I had been awarded my Doctorate (my real one, I mean; not the honorary one I got the Stadhouder to demand for me) but old habits die hard and people still commonly referred to me as Master Mercurius. I was firmly embedded in the Faculty of Theology and Rectors had stopped trying to remove me. After my last adventure in the service of the Stadhouder, William had left me in peace for a while. I would love to think that this was recognition of the fact that he had put my life in peril through one of his uniquely hare-brained schemes, but I doubt that he was aware of that or would have cared if he had been. William would risk his life for his country and expected no less of the rest of us. Of course, if we lesser mortals risk ours, he won't need to risk his.

To be fair to him, he had offered me an apartment in The Hague and a stipend so that I would not need to work at the University of Leiden and could be available to him at a moment's notice. He seemed to think that this was an attraction of the offer, rather than a major drawback as I saw it. It would have been delightful to see the Princess Mary more often. I esteemed her qualities very highly; she was an intelligent, observant and kindly woman who just happened to be an atrocious speller. There was no impropriety between us, nor could there be; she was devoted to her husband the Stadhouder, and he to her; he kept one or two mistresses but spent hardly any time with them and to be honest his heart was not really in adultery. The Princess was very much a one-man woman, and as for the rest of us, any inclination to fornication with her was dampened by the certain knowledge that a man who seduced her would soon be spending a very uncomfortable afternoon strapped to a table while William personally removed his genitalia.

Anyway, I only wanted to be a lecturer at the University. It was my proudest moment when I was given the job and I am still here. I teach quite rarely now, partly because I am eighty-three years old and prone to nod off if the room is too warm, so my days are filled by sitting here dictating my memories to my clerk. That is how I have spent the last four years, and, God willing, I will do so until Death comes calling. [Van der Meer just said he hopes that Death will not come for several years yet. I'm not expecting Death to visit soon — after all, Van der Meer looks to be in good health, if one overlooks the curious snorting noises he makes when I am dictating.]

Now, where was I? Oh, yes, the spring of 1686. The one cloud under which I laboured was that I still had to lecture to undergraduates a few times a year. Talk about casting your pearls before swine (Matthew, chapter 7, verse 6).

Leiden, The Feast of St Polycarp, 1722.

CHAPTER ONE

When the door was opened we could see the victim lying there in the middle of the floor, face down but with his head turned slightly to the left, and the blood around it formed a ghastly halo that told us he was very much a dead man.

I am bound to admit that I was relieved that the victim was not someone else, which was unworthy of me. Even the most unpleasant of people does not deserve to be struck down in so brutal a fashion. It was true that I had thought him an unmannerly boor, an untrustworthy witness, an unchristian soul and that I was not alone in thinking that. No doubt the murderer had thought along similar lines. But if I made a list of those who probably thought that way it did nothing to reduce the length of the list of candidate killers, because it seemed to be almost a universal view.

I apologise, of course, to any relatives of his who might be reading this. It must be painful to discover that you are descended from such a repulsive character.

[What's that, Van der Meer? What do you mean, who was he?]

Ah, I am getting ahead of myself again. You, dear reader, cannot know of whom I am speaking. Nor, for that matter, have I adequately explained why I was in Maastricht in the first place, instead of sitting in the warmth of Steen's Inn with a beaker of beer and a good book, where I would have infinitely preferred to be.

I suppose I ought to start at the beginning, if I can remember what the beginning was. Let's go back to the day when the idea of the trip was first mooted.

7

[Get fresh paper, Van der Meer. We'll start again.]

Oh, I remember now. What an awful morning that was.

I felt in need of a drink.

Actually, I felt in need of about six drinks in the hope that kindly oblivion would overpower me and I would forget the last couple of hours.

Maybe I was becoming less tolerant as the years pass. Alternatively, maybe our undergraduates were becoming less and less gifted.

An education at the University of Leiden is, of course, much sought after. The problem is that some of our young men just want to be able to say that they attended the University for a while. They have no thought of taking a degree, which is just as well because they have as much chance of graduating as I have of hopping to The Hague.

Let us at least begin this book with some good news. After getting me jailed and condemned to death with one of his byzantine little schemes, the Stadhouder, William of Orange, had been very quiet lately and had not required my help for the best part of a year. This met with my entire approval; indeed, I was hoping it would continue for some time, ideally until my retirement. I was forty-seven years old, and not suited to climbing out of prisons on a rope or rowing at sea, both of which had recently been necessary. My normal daily exercise involved a brisk walk to the inn on the Langebrug and some heavy-duty page turning in the library. I am a gentleman of settled and sedentary habits.

I loved Leiden. I had lived there since I first arrived as a student over thirty years before, and never wanted to be anywhere else, though this resolve had been tested lately because Albrecht, our kitchen master, had somehow laid his hands on a French cookery book and was now able to marry his incendiary gifts with a variety of revolting sauces. He recently gave us a jug of mustard sauce and a jug of custard and none of us was able to identify which was which with any certainty, even after we tasted each.

I was also very proud of my association with the finest university in the United Provinces, if not the world; a pride which others were like to prey on, to my disadvantage.

I had posed a simple problem to my ethics class. Let us suppose that someone has given you a sum of money, but you realise that it is a mistake, and the money should have gone to another. What should you do about it?

This was intended to be a ten-minute discussion to break the ice and encourage class participation before I moved on to weightier matters. I had no idea that two hours later none of my students would have even tentatively suggested that the money should be given back. I was still having difficulty explaining to one that my question was entirely hypothetical, and I was not in a position to lend him ten guilders from the payment that I had received.

Thus battered intellectually, I staggered from the room and wondered if it was too early to go to the inn. Since our day starts at seven o'clock, it was not yet mid-morning, but there were extenuating circumstances, and I had no further lectures that day, so I was just heading for my chamber to collect my cloak when I was intercepted by the Rector.

'Ah, Mercurius! We are well met.'

'Indeed, Rector?'

'Indeed. I have a little matter I should like to discuss with you if you are at leisure for half an hour.'

I toyed with telling him that I had an urgent appointment with a small barrel of ale, but I doubt Wolferdus Senguerdius would have been impressed. When you work in a university you are accustomed to meeting men of great achievements, but even in this setting Senguerdius was extraordinarily stellar. So far as I could make out, he took his Doctorate in Philosophy at the age of 21 and became a fellow lecturer in philosophy. I cannot say that we were close; he did not socialize, preferring to spend his time writing impenetrable theses. By the age of 30 he was Professor of Natural Philosophy and, as if that were not enough, he picked up a Doctorate in Law from the University of Utrecht. The one thing he seemed not to have collected along the way was a sense of humour.

He wrapped an arm around my shoulders like a particularly disreputable uncle about to suggest a carouse. 'Come now, Mercurius. A glass of wine?'

'It's a little early for me, Rector,' I said.

He made no move to fetch himself a glass. 'Well, sit you down. It is a matter that touches upon the honour and reputation of the University, Mercurius, which I know you hold very dear.'

He was right there.

'I have received a letter,' he said, holding it up but not allowing me to read it. 'It is from the University of Leuven. They wish to propose a friendly debate between our two universities.'

I could have done with that wine now. The idea of a "friendly" debate between universities makes no sense at all. It is like sentencing someone to a polite disembowelling. Believe me, most university staff don't know the meaning of friendly debate. I have known some who would have sold their own mothers into whoredom if it enabled them to make a good point.

Leuven, or Louvain if you prefer the French version of the name, is in the Southern provinces, a bit less than a day's walk to the east of Brussels. There is a certain amount of rivalry between us, because Leiden is an institution of the Reformed faith, whereas Leuven is very much a Roman Catholic university.

'You will be aware, Mercurius, that there is some rivalry between us. We cannot allow ourselves to be beaten in this encounter.'

'You propose to accept the challenge, Rector?'

'Of course. It would be unmanly to decline it. Besides, I'm quite looking forward to it.'

'You'll lead our team?'

'Mercurius, kindly suppress that tone of surprise in your voice.'

'I'm sorry. I meant only that with your other duties...'

'I'm sure the University won't miss me for a few days.'

It was time to broach the subject that was hanging over me. 'And you're telling me this because...?'

'I want you to be the other member of the Leiden team, Mercurius. Oh, I know there are others with a more impressive list of publications, but you have a certain flexibility of mind.'

I had brought one question to the fore, but that just raised another one, and to explain that I need to go back a bit.

As I said, Leiden is a Reformed institution. To teach theology or philosophy you are supposed to be a member of the Reformed Church, and ideally a minister — which I am. The snag is that in 1664 I converted to Catholicism and was ordained as a Catholic priest, but it suited my bishop to keep this fact secret, because he feared an outbreak of anti-Catholic feeling and wanted some priests up his sleeve to reconstitute the Church if they were needed. Of course, it suited me too, because it meant I could keep my job at Leiden.

However, because there were no bishops in the United Provinces at the time, and for the sake of secrecy, I was ordained by the Bishop of Namur, also in the Southern provinces, and it was to him that I was answerable. Thereby hangs a tale.

In 1684, he summoned me to visit him. Unfortunately I was on a mission for the Stadhouder at the time, and since I didn't fancy a long trip to Namur, I persuaded William to show his appreciation of my efforts by banning me from leaving the country, which was the reason I gave the bishop for my non-attendance. I had, in fact, been to England since, but with luck the bishop would know nothing of that. The ban was still in force but I could certainly have it lifted so I could go to Leuven; the difficulty was that it would look very odd if I went there but not to see my bishop. In fact, given that the University of Leuven would probably invite him to be in the audience, it could all be very awkward. It would be much better if I could get out of going.

'Where do they propose to hold this debate?' I asked.

'That is open to discussion,' Senguerdius replied. 'They have offered to host it, but are equally willing to come here.'

That sounded a much better arrangement.

'But,' he continued, 'to require them to do so seems to me to be abusing their generosity. More to the point, if they lose, as they inevitably will, it may tarnish our victory if we had the advantage of being at home.'

This desire for fair play, while entirely laudable, was unlikely to be reciprocated. I know what I'm talking about. I have studied alongside Jesuits, who would not scruple to stoop to anything that guaranteed them a win. They might even poison our food; though, come to think of it, after years of eating the cooking of our kitchen master Albrecht we were probably immune to any poison known to man.

'How about Aachen?' I suggested.

Senguerdius appeared shocked. 'You're an innocent when it comes to politics, aren't you, Mercurius?'

Needless to say, instead of just telling me what I didn't know, Senguerdius subjected me to a ten-minute diatribe about the perfidy of the Archbishop of Cologne, in whose diocese Aachen sits. While it was geographically perfect, being just outside our borders in one of the German princedoms, there was the small matter of the Franco-Dutch War to consider.

The intelligent reader may, like me, wonder what a German city has to do with the Franco-Dutch War which had, in any event, ended nearly a decade earlier. The point is that we could have fought off the French advancing through the Southern provinces. We had a defensive line prepared. It was the Archbishop of Cologne's decision to invite the French army to march through his lands and then attack us from the east that put my country in such peril, and many Dutchmen have not forgotten or forgiven this. After all, his motive for doing so was that the French had offered him a chunk of our eastern lands to annex to his. It was a purely mercenary action on his part.

The said intelligent reader might also be wondering what sort of churchman would do such a thing. The answer is Maximilian Henry of Bavaria, who was one of the younger sons of a German nobleman and whose uncle happened to be the previous Archbishop of Cologne. I know some people are prodigies, but when you consider that Maximilian Henry was given a job by his uncle and succeeded to the Archbishopric at the age of 28, not to mention becoming Bishop of Hildesheim and Bishop of Liège, you cannot help feeling that nepotism may have been involved. For a start it has been established since at least the Council of Trent (1545–1563, since you're asking) that a candidate for bishop must be over thirty years old, and however you do the sums, Maximilian Henry was not.

The papacy got round this using a process called postulation, in which the Church authorities of a diocese write to the Pope saying "We know he isn't 30 years old, but we think X would make a great bishop for us, and, by the way, here is a chest of money to cover your expenses in investigating the matter. Don't bother with a receipt." This process was made easier in the case of Cologne by the fact that Maximilian Henry was the senior cleric after the dead Archbishop, so he was able to write the letter himself. [Van der Meer is asking me whether anyone is at all interested in this guff. No, of course they aren't. But if I don't explain it they won't understand why Senguerdius would not entertain Aachen as a venue. Anyway, Van der Meer's job is to write down what I say, or as close to it as he can manage, not to offer criticisms.]

The next option we came up with was Breda. It is a fine city, and roughly halfway between Leiden and Leuven. Moreover, there was a disused College there that might have made a good venue; the *Scola Illustris et Collegium Auriacum*, commonly called the Orange College because a Stadhouder had set it up, had finally run out of impetus in 1669 and been closed. I had no idea what had become of its buildings, but there was sure to be somewhere suitable in a place like Breda.

The drawback with Breda is that it had been part of the Prince of Orange-Nassau's personal lands for centuries. Nowhere in our country was there a stronger attachment to the Stadhouder than there. There were bound to be questions about whether we would be allowed to lose there, or escape unscathed if we did. If I had been a Leuven team member I would have objected to Breda as insufficiently neutral.

'Leave it with me,' Senguerdius said. 'I'll write to accept the challenge and ask them to suggest some possible venues.'

'And how will the topic be chosen?' I asked.

'Ah, didn't I say? They've already suggested one. "That the sin in witchcraft is to be imputed to idolatry." What do you make of that, Mercurius?'

Any attempt to compress the arguments of centuries into a paragraph or two must be bound to fail, but Leuven's suggested question was a good one insofar as it pointed to a difference of opinion that might be expected to separate Catholics from Protestants.

Contrary to public belief, witchcraft trials are not all an invention of the Roman Catholic Church, though some Popes have occasionally promoted them. While we might differ about which magical powers are really possessed by witches and sorcerers and which are not, a lot of Roman Catholics are disposed to believe that witchcraft is real, that some people have some magical powers, and that they obtain these by enslaving themselves to Satan. Now, if they are worshipping Satan, they are infringing the very first of the Ten Commandments which instructs us that "You shall have no other gods before Me", which is idolatry, hence the framing of the motion Leuven wanted to debate.

There would have been plenty of Protestants who would have agreed with this proposition. How else could one explain the witch burnings in England and Scotland within my lifetime? Nor was this a matter of mere historical interest; if reports were to be credited, witch trials were still proceeding in the Americas.

On the other hand, we Dutch are a tolerant people, and, on balance, we like our opinions to be supported by facts; and it was a fact that I had never seen a case of witchcraft reported that was undoubtedly due to supernatural causes. If a man claims his neighbour has made him impotent we are allowed to ask how often he visits the alehouse. If cheese refuses to set, well, let us recall that occasionally that happened to my grandmother, but she never thought it was anything other than a defect in the milk or rennet.

In short, many of us hold to the rational explanation that the sin in witchcraft is one of fraud. People are claiming to have and use powers that, in fact, they do not have, thereby taking advantage of their gullible neighbours.

Intellectually, I felt no scruples about attacking the debate proposition. As an ordinary human being, I was rather more concerned that if the debate were to take place in the Catholic Southern provinces, anyone who denied the reality of witchcraft might find himself accused of providing cover for witches or being a witch himself. Just because I feel the cold does not mean that I would find standing on a bunch of burning embers congenial.

CHAPTER TWO

As I age I find that a great many of the plans others make do not come to fruition, so having been added, involuntarily, to the University of Leiden debating team I immediately forgot about it and got on with my work.

Readers may recall that I have occasionally made mention of my illustrious predecessor Adriaan Heereboord. Heereboord was a generation before me, a bold and modern thinker, who held the Chair of Philosophy at Leiden from the age of thirty. If you know that the word "symposium" was originally defined as a drinking party, it will not surprise you to know that Heereboord was fond of a flask or two, after which his cogitations became more daring and outspoken. As a result of this predilection he fell out with almost everyone, stopped lecturing and eventually died when he was only 47.

His name has something of a cloud over it now, but I sat at his feet, figuratively and literally, and he could be quite brilliant when he was thinking clearly. Even when he wasn't, he was capable of flashes of insight. I recall an occasion when he extemporised a verse response to Jacobus Revius, an austere Calvinist theologian-poet, while lying on his back on a tavern floor. It was not, perhaps, suitable for publication, nor anatomically accurate, but it neatly demolished one of Revius' arguments.

Anyway, Heereboord had written a book called *Collegium ethicum* which collated his ideas about an ethical system. It had not received much attention for nearly forty years, but when I re-read it I realised that there were parallels with my own work on Aristotle's *Nicomachean Ethics*, with which, no doubt, my readers are entirely familiar. However, writers counter the opposing arguments of their day, so while Aristotle and Heereboord said some similar things, they said them in slightly different ways to deal with their adversaries' criticisms, and since so long had elapsed since Heereboord's publication it occurred to me that there might be new arguments on both sides that should be investigated.

Accordingly, I was sitting in Steen's inn on the Langebrug with a copy of Heereboord's work open before me and a beaker of ale to my left where I was less likely to knock it over while scribbling. Using my left hand to hold the beaker meant I could continue to write while drinking.

The door opened and Little Gerrit came in, blinking to accustom his eyes to the relative darkness. Silhouetted against the open doorway, he was not immediately recognisable, but the smell of fish was the first thing I noticed.

Gerrit was a kitchen boy at the University whose job was to receive deliveries of the food that Albrecht proposed to ruin in the ovens and stow it in the appropriate storeroom until it was needed. When items were needed in a hurry he would be sent to run the errand, all of which he did in exchange for his keep and a bed by the large oven. It was his job to ensure that the fire did not burn down at night, something which was not in his interest either given that he was sleeping beside it. He was a cheerful lad and seemed quite content with his lot, although he never had much money, so upon seeing him I reached into my pouch to find some coppers for a drink for the boy.

Seeing me, he smiled and ran to take the stool across the table.

'Good day, Master,' he said brightly, displaying a surprisingly good set of teeth for someone who subsisted entirely on Albrecht's cooking; still, he was young yet.

'Good day, Gerrit,' I replied. 'Will you have a drink with me?'

He looked suddenly anxious. 'I would, Master, but I don't think we have time.'

'We?'

'Well, you, really.'

'Why me?'

'The Rector has asked me to tell you he has had a reply from Liv — no, Lerp —'

'Leuven?'

'That's the man. Anyway, he would like to see you as soon as he can.'

I nodded. 'Well, he's not here, is he?'

'No, Master.'

'So he can't see me at the moment.'

'No, Master.'

'So I've got time to finish my drink. And you can at least have a small one so I'm not drinking alone.'

The boy brightened again, and gleefully accepted, cradling his beaker with both hands and savouring the fresh beer within. Occasionally people wonder that quite young people drink beer in Leiden, which just proves that they have never attempted to drink the water. While our canals are undoubtedly picturesque, they accumulate the detritus of the city despite the severe penalties if you are caught polluting them. Curiously, Dutchmen do not often urinate in them, not so much from a concern for public hygiene as in the knowledge that drunk men all too often fall in and perish there, but foreigners are regularly denounced to the authorities for such acts. No, the chief source of the unwholesomeness of the water is the wool trade, because the washings from the fleeces find their way into the canals and cause a vile scum to pool on the surface.

A few minutes later, Gerrit and I strolled back to the academy building together, though he detached himself to enter at the back door since he knew his place. I, on the other hand, had the privilege of entering at the front. Seeing me approaching with Heereboord's book in my arms one of the porters rushed to open the door for me, which made me feel very grand, an illusion shattered when I skidded on the mat just inside the door and finished up sitting on the floor in an undignified manner.

I brushed myself down and ascended the staircase. Senguerdius liked to work with his door open. He chose to present this as evidence of his approachability, but I think it owed rather more to his desire to see what was going on in the corridor.

Anyway, as a result, he saw me before I was able to knock, and beckoned me to enter.

'You wished to see me, Rector?'

'Yes, that's why I sent for you. Above a quarter of an hour ago.'

'I'm sorry, I did not appreciate the urgency of your message.'

Senguerdius smiled. It was a smile at once wide and insincere. His lips twitched as if rebelling at being forced into an unnatural act.

'Never mind that now. Sit down, Mercurius.' He waved a piece of paper at me. 'A further letter from Leuven! We have agreed a date and place for our great triumph, Mercurius.'

Whatever qualities Senguerdius may have lacked, self-confidence was not one of them.

'Indeed, Rector?'

'Indeed, Mercurius! First, as to date. We are to meet on the Monday after Pentecost.'

You might think that a priest such as myself would have no trouble remembering the date of Pentecost, but it keeps moving. Fortunately I had it written down.

'That's Monday, 3rd June,' Senguerdius helpfully glossed.

'And where?'

'In the Emperor's Hall of the Basilica of Saint Servatius, in Maastricht.'

My heart may have skipped a beat here, and not in rapture. Now that the French army had finally been induced to leave, the city of Maastricht was once more in Dutch hands, but it must have been twice as far from Leiden to Maastricht as it was from Leuven to Maastricht. Maastricht is also a predominantly Roman Catholic city. I could not help feeling that Senguerdius' confidence had led him to accept a number of matters to our disadvantage.

Then there is the matter of language. When pushed, most of the educated people in Maastricht can speak Dutch. Given that Aachen is close at hand, many of them also speak German; but left to their own devices they speak their own barbarous Limburger dialect. Try to imagine a drunk Englishman attempting to converse in Dutch — actually, not something that many of us have to imagine, since drunk Englishmen are commonplace — and you will have some idea what Limburger dialect sounds like.

'The Archbishop of Cologne is, unfortunately, unable to be present,' Senguerdius continued.

I bet he would have been if there was money involved, I thought, but decided to say nothing.

'In his absence, his auxiliary bishop, Johann Heinrich von Anethan, will preside.'

I knew of him by reputation, which was of an honest, hard-working priest, the one who actually did the work of the diocese while his Archbishop played politics and counted his money. Nevertheless, he was a Roman Catholic bishop; but I suppose in a dispute between a Protestant university and a Roman Catholic one it must be quite difficult to find someone neutral. There are a few Jews about, but I fear that a Jewish president would merely draw abuse from both sides.

'Then, as to the jury; each university will select three men of learning with no connection with their university from a list of those working in Germany. Well, clearly, Mercurius, we'll pick three Protestants and they'll pick three Catholics. The president doesn't get a vote, by the way. One team will speak on days one and three, and the other on days two and four; no address is to exceed eight hours.'

Thank goodness for small mercies, I thought. I have never spoken for eight hours straight in my life, and this was not the time to start.

'We'll have to discuss whether I'm better opening for us or closing the debate. There is much to be said for each option.'

'Surely you should open, Rector,' I said. This was not idle flattery; this way, if he made any good points I could steal them and incorporate them in my address. In the outside world this is called plagiarism, but in a university it is known as research.

'You think so? Well, it would get us off to a flying start, I suppose. Let's come back to that.'

I trudged back to my room feeling rather downcast. In just a handful of weeks we would be setting out on a miserable journey right across the country to the south-east. I expected that we would make our way south to Rotterdam and then by river upstream to Maastricht. Depending on the way the river was running it could be three to four days' travel each way, the journeys being separated by a miserable week. And if Senguerdius picked the wrong type of Protestant for the jury we could even lose — and I was in no illusions about which member of the team would be blamed for any defeat we might suffer.

[Van der Meer thinks I should explain what I mean by "the wrong type of Protestant". Really?]

The problem is that the one thing everyone knows about Protestants is that they protest, but they don't all protest about the same things, so within less than two centuries they have fragmented into a wide range of denominations differing on a number of points of doctrine. I cannot remember them all, but readers may have heard of Martin Luther in Wittenberg, who offered to debate allcomers on no less than 95 grumbles about the Roman Catholic Church that he had nailed on a church door.

In no time, another fellow called Zwingli had made his mark in Zürich, complaining that monks and bishops were living dissolute and greedy lives, and that Luther had not gone far enough in his criticisms. John Calvin, a Frenchman living in Geneva, thought the same, but he had a different list of complaints to Zwingli (who was dead by then anyway).

On top of these, there were the Anabaptists, groups who believed that infants cannot consent to baptism which should therefore be delayed until they are of mature years. The great achievement of the Anabaptists was to unite everyone else against them, and in any history of the Church you will observe that the leaders of most of these sects enjoyed relatively short lives and usually ended up on the gallows or at the stake. Lately some of them have decided to emigrate to the Americas where, I note, they quickly make themselves reviled by all they meet and new persecutions result.

For myself, I have no truck with Anabaptist doctrines but I feel some admiration for the willingness of new men to come forward in the stead of those who have been martyred. By contrast, in my church we have men turning down bishoprics because they can't afford to take a pay cut, having found themselves a collection of nice little swindles that keep them in luxury. I could tell you a story about a German bishop and his "niece" that would make your ears burn with disgust (if you understood some of the things they got up to, that is). I have nothing against mortification of the flesh as a pious practice, but usually you scourge yourself with a little whip, rather than employing hired prostitutes to strip naked to do it for you.

I had found a little book on witchcraft and its detection in our University library, though I have no idea why we had it there, and I opened it again and continued to read, until my thoughts were disturbed by that list of Germans who were to form the jury. Surely, you might think, if the debate was only a few weeks away it was a bit late to send invitations to sit on the jury? After all, there was barely time for the invitations to be sent and replies received before the debate started.

Ah, but you misapprehend the interests of those invited! University professors spend much of their lives hoping to pick up this kind of invitation, and when one comes they will drop everything to get there. Having arrived, they will take care to be seen by everyone who matters, which increases the chances that another invitation will come their way; they will introduce themselves to mayors and bishops, and try to wangle an invitation to some fashionable party; they will mercilessly flatter ladies who may have some social influence; and they will add it to their *curriculum vitae* as evidence that they are learned men whose opinions are courted.

It is possible that a professor might turn down an invitation on the grounds that he would have to miss his wedding, or a parent's funeral clashed with the date (though even then they would keep their mother's corpse above ground for a few extra days rather than miss a conference). Anyway, the chances are that the two sides had been lining up their judges for some time, so they would have been sounded out about their availability already, in which case there was no point in my wasting any effort on it.

I regret to say that my mind wandered, and I found myself considering why Senguerdius was not in the library too. Did he plan to do no research? He was one of those extremely irritating sorts who rarely need to read anything twice to remember it. Either that, or he was an exceptional bluffer who relied upon the opponent not having closely read the book that he had just offered as evidence for his contention. This happens more than you might suppose in academia. Nobody has access to all the books ever written, and even the most celebrated author occasionally produces a volume of nonsense, but the chances are that very few will have read it, so just mentioning their name is good enough. I, for example, have read every book by St Thomas Aquinas that I have been able to find, but I know of at least two that I have never seen. Were I so minded, I could probably quote those two books in the debate and make claims about their content in the hope that the other team would not have read them either. The problem would be if there were a copy in the Leuven University library.

The little book was very depressing. It treated of the Roermond witch trials of 1613 — you have to specify the date because witch trials seem to have been quite frequent in Roermond. This may have been because accusations of sorcery were very simply made there. If you thought you had been bewitched you confronted the supposed witch and demanded that they lift the spell with a blessing. If they refused to do so you denounced them as a contumacious witch who had refused to undo the harm that they had done because they obviously wished you ill-will; but if they agreed, this was interpreted as a tacit admission that they had caused the harm in the first place, so they could expect to be burned.

Some of the evidence was quite laughable if the consequences had not been so serious for the accused, and it is hard to understand how men of any intelligence could have accepted this rubbish.

The first "witches" arrested were a mother and daughter who were conjurors. The daughter showed her friends that she could make coins appear and disappear, producing coppers from her mouth or ears. This was observed by a magistrate who saw it as clear evidence of witchcraft; never mind that you could see such things at almost any fair. Once at the goose fair I saw a man put three eggs in his mouth, one after another, and it never crossed my mind that he was a sorcerer, though I still have no idea how he did it. Anyway, the girl was condemned to a convent for life, while her mother was burned alive. She had allegedly confessed to killing 41 children and 10 adults with her magic.

Now, the odd thing is that 41 children must be a substantial proportion of those born in Roermond and the mothers must, one assumes, have been known to the "witch", because you don't bewitch people you don't know. Yet I could find no evidence that anyone thought that there was anything unusual about these infants' deaths until after the woman confessed.

Unfortunately, babies die. Given the miserable conditions in which some have to live, this is hardly surprising. The poor woman, Trijntje van Zittaert, was tortured to cause her to confess. In my service of our Stadhouder William, I had seen his torture master Beniamino at work, and I am fairly sure that he could get anyone to confess to anything with a little bit of effort. Goodness knows, as soon as he unrolled the pouch containing the tools of his trade my hands went clammy, and I wasn't the one strapped to the chair looking at the pliers and pincers.

As a priest I occasionally have to hear confessions, and the sins detailed there may be an impediment to eternal life in Heaven, so you might think that people would be keen to unburden themselves, yet I hear far less in an hour at confession than Beniamino could elicit in ten minutes just by starting a fire and leaving a few pokers in it to warm up. Maybe priests should try leaving a brazier beside the Confessional?

CHAPTER THREE

If there has been any advantage to my service for the Stadhouder (apart, of course, from any fee that he may have given me) it is that I have learned to pack for trips. The untutored reader might suppose that as a clergyman my choice of clothes is fairly restricted, and they would be absolutely right. It usually takes me no more than a couple of hours to pack my clothes and razor. The difficult part is deciding what books to take.

When travelling alone I read voraciously, and can usually manage thirty pages an hour or so, meaning that I need to take quite a few books. Expecting to be in Maastricht about a week that set an upper limit of seven books; but then I would be travelling with the Rector, who might well want to talk, so maybe I would need fewer. On the other hand, there were one or two books I might need for reference, particularly about witchcraft. During the afternoon I think I may have packed up to thirty-five volumes, taken many back out again, and gone to the library to find one or two more, and finally closed my chest with eleven inside.

I was somewhat disconcerted to see the Rector supervising a couple of porters who were trying to manhandle two chests down the stairs to the main door.

'Travelling light, Mercurius? I hope you have your doctoral robes in there.'

I had not. It had not crossed my mind that I might need them.

'We've got to put on a bit of a show, Mercurius. Make them realise they're not dealing with country bumpkins. We're every bit as good as they are.'

'Isn't it more important that our arguments should be better?' I grumbled.

'Well, yes, that too. But take it from me, Mercurius, you can get a head start over them with a few little tactics.'

These "little tactics" were explained to me over the first part of the journey, as we took a barge to Rotterdam.

'Keep the judges in your eye. Don't favour the opponents with even a fleeting glance. If they stumble over their words, do a bit of coughing so they can't correct themselves. If you're got a gown with big sleeves, wear it while you're speaking. It makes you look more stately. And when you reach your main argument, extend both arms so you look bigger and more imposing. There's a reason why ravens extend their wings before they try to peck your eyes out. Have you brought any books?'

'Several, Rector.'

'Excellent! Keep one open in front of you, and if your argument is weak in some part, pick the book up and give them the impression that you're reading directly from it.'

'But suppose the book says nothing germane to the matter?'

'They won't know that, Mercurius. Unless one of them actually wrote the book, I suppose, so make sure that they have no opportunity to see what you're reading.'

'And if I'm asked?'

'If your opponents ask, ignore them. If the judges ask, just give the author without any details as to the particular book you have before you.'

How naïve was I? I had supposed we were going to better any adversaries by the force of our arguments, but Senguerdius was more interested in victory by any means. I felt rather as if we were taking a pack of marked cards into a game while keeping an ace in each sleeve just in case.

'You needn't look so po-faced, Mercurius. Do you suppose that our opponents are doing anything different to us? They do this debating all the time so they'll know the full range of tricks. They'll pack the hall with their supporters to applaud on cue with a view to influencing the judges. When they come up against the eight-hour limit they'll just keep talking. They'll interrupt and then apologise profusely when we've lost the thread of our argument.'

I had to admit that if there were Jesuits in the Leuven team these were exactly the kind of things we ought to expect. Not long after I was ordained I happened to be at an abbey in France when the new prior was being elected and the shenanigans that went on then would have shamed a cathouse. I ought not to single out the Jesuits; for all I know they may be models of probity compared with other societies and orders. But I cannot help feeling there is a reason why they were kicked out of Venice 80 years ago during a tiff with the Papacy and not allowed back for 50 years after the fuss had blown over.

'Now, as to the judges,' Senguerdius continued, 'I think I have pulled off quite a coup there. Leuven have, of course, selected three particularly dull Germans, all Catholics. Fortunately that did not restrict my choice, because there are plenty of dull Germans to go round. But I have found us a gem, Mercurius!'

'Indeed, Rector. Who is he?'

Senguerdius produced a smile so wide I feared the top half of his head might fall off. 'Not he, Mercurius; she!'

'A woman?'

'That's when the pronoun "she" is normally used, is it not?'

'But who?'

I would not have my readers, particularly any of the fair sex, believe that I have any prejudice against the intelligence of women. Far from it; I have known many gifted and learned ladies. I believe I have previously mentioned the celebrated Anna Maria van Schurman who was a painter, writer and musician and could speak fourteen languages. Then there was Argula von Grumbach, who offered to dispute with the entire faculty of the University of Ingolstadt in support of Luther's Protestant views. And I have made clear my admiration of the Princess Mary, a woman of uncommon good sense and wide learning, once you could decipher her spelling.

'Have you heard of the Freiin Mathilde von Burghalter?'

'No,' I answered shortly.

'You may, perhaps, be better acquainted with her older sister, Freiin Dorothea?'

'No.'

'Well,' he answered good-humouredly, 'I suppose you don't get out much.'

If it was up to me I wouldn't get out at all, I thought, *except for the occasional toddle to Steen's inn.*

'Freiin Dorothea was perhaps not conventionally beautiful,' Senguerdius continued, using that phrase that polite people use to describe a woman who has a face like a horse's rear end, 'but she had a very large dowry as there were no surviving men in her family.'

That makes a woman more attractive in the view of many men. Expensive diamond earrings attract the eye and distract you from the face.

'Unfortunately Dorothea was unlucky in love. Her first husband had a riding accident, if I remember correctly, while the second made a terrible error in a battle and was killed along with most of the men from his estates. Anyway, that's not the point. Her younger sister, Mathilde, rejected wealth and position and entered a convent where she is now Abbess. I am told her mystical poetry is very striking. You may know her as Abbess Mathilde, the Prophetess of Hope.'

Now, I had heard of *her*. I had read some of her pamphlets, not without profit.

'Forgive me, Rector, but isn't she another Catholic?'

'Well, yes, technically,' he replied testily, 'but she's a woman, Mercurius! She'll be so grateful to us for inviting her to this she's bound to be sympathetic. Women don't get these honours every day, you know.'

I was sure that he was right, but not quite so sure that Abbess Mathilde would be shallow enough to have her head turned by an unexpected invitation. Far be it from me to argue with my superiors [Van der Meer just asked me to repeat that to check that he had heard it correctly, the impudent scoundrel] but my limited experience of women is that many of the kindly acts men show towards them are regarded as evidence of male condescension — which they often are, women being, for the most part, good judges of men's motives and character — and therefore they fail to soften the womanly heart.

I recall a student some years ago who was enamoured of a wool merchant's daughter and nearly bankrupted himself to buy her a pair of garnet and pearl earrings, only to be rejected by the girl on the grounds of profligacy because he should, if his intentions were honest, have been saving his money for their future life together. The student admitted ruefully that there was some force in this argument, or would have been if he had ever spoken to her about marriage, but since her mother was always in the room when they were together the opportunity had not arisen. He sold the rejected jewellery at a loss and used the proceeds to get drunk, as a result of which he fell in a canal and drowned; at which point, of course, the young lady erupted in tears and confined herself to her room, believing that he had romantically done away with himself as a result of his spurned love.

'Who are our other judges, Rector?' I enquired, hoping that he had shown more judgement with these.

'There's an old student from Leiden called Ehrenfried Walther von Tschirnhaus. A Saxon, I believe, from the far east of the country, but a brilliant mathematician and a well-connected philosopher.'

'Forgive me, but how will his mathematics assist us?'

'Oh, he probably won't listen to the evidence. He's far too busy writing a large work, or so he told me, but I persuaded him to come anyway. He likes meeting interesting people. That won't get him far with his fellow judges, but he'll meet you and me.'

'And the third one?'

'Ah, there I have been rather cunning. Around 50 years ago there was a great witch-craze in the city of Bamberg. I happen to know a local historian, Dr Jakob Pfeiffer, who has made an extensive study of the records and has written a book arguing that there was never any such thing as witchcraft. He probably won't listen to the arguments either because he knows it all.'

I did not choose to make the point audibly, but it seemed to me that our strategy here was simple, namely to select three judges, one of whom would be flattered to have been invited and two of whom would not bother themselves with the evidence, thus ensuring three votes and at least a tie. This seemed a flimsy foundation for our success.

Against that, I had been doing a little research of my own, and I had to admit that Senguerdius had a very good record in debates, and in some of those he would have had no say in the judges or format. And against that, a little voice inside my head kept reminding me that if we failed it would undoubtedly be recorded as a Mercurius failure rather than a team failure, because there was only one candidate for scapegoat. If you have forgotten the account of the scapegoat in the Bible, you will find it in Leviticus, chapter 16: 'After he hath cleansed the sanctuary, and the tabernacle, and the altar, then let him offer the living goat: and putting both hands upon his head, let him confess all the iniquities of the children of Israel, and all their offences and sins: and praying that they may light on his head, he shall turn him out by a man ready for it, into the desert.'

Which is all very well for the children of Israel, but pretty tough on the blameless goat, in my opinion. But if we lost the debate, I was as certain as I could be that Senguerdius would adopt the role of high priest and cast me as the goat, which may explain why my sympathies lay where they did.

At Rotterdam, Senguerdius announced that time was tight before we caught our next barge, which would take us to a little place called Rossum, where we would cross to the Maas river for the third stage of our journey. What Senguerdius actually meant was that there would only be time for a small feast and a couple of bottles of wine before the barge left, and I am quite certain that if the money spent on lunch had been offered to the bargemaster it would have left at any time that pleased us.

I confess that I had little appetite. I rarely have. My habit is to eat sparingly and I am usually content with some bread and cheese or ham, possibly a result of prolonged exposure to Albrecht's "cooking". His incinerated cuisine would curb anyone's gluttony.

I would happily have eaten in silence, but Senguerdius was as voluble as ever. We lecturers talk; it is what we do for a living, so silent professors are rare birds. But even by the standards of the University, Senguerdius stood out. He had knowledge of almost any subject, and an opinion about many more, so I had little to do to keep up my end of the conversation. All that was required of me was to mutter "Really?" or "You don't say" when he stopped to breathe.

As I recall, he was busy explaining the defects of the Peace of Westphalia to me (he was two years old when it was signed) when the bargemaster appeared at our table clutching his cap in an agitated manner and explained that if the barge did not leave soon he would lose his fee for carrying some items of commerce. Senguerdius, always alert to the struggles of the working man, at once agreed that we must leave without delay and, pausing only to pay the bill and fill a napkin with the remains of a chicken, he wrapped his cloak about him and strode to the door.

If the alert reader has divined that I was not enjoying this journey he (or she) may imagine how I felt half an hour later when the skies opened and the contents of Heaven tumbled about our heads. I am told that rain is nature's way of replenishing our rivers, in which case we were in no danger of the Rijn drying up. It was as if all of God's angels had decided to have a pee at the same time.

It was impossible to read, for our books would have been ruined, so I decided to think about something or other. Looking about me for inspiration, I soon realised that there is not much to see on a barge, but fell to regarding my fellow passengers to see what I might infer from their appearance.

There was a large, self-satisfied looking man for a start. He wore an old-fashioned black sugarloaf hat with a silver buckle, and, despite the inclement weather, gazed steadily behind us. Regret at leaving somewhere? His eyes were rheumy and prominent, and his cheeks were highly coloured, suggestive of an overexuberant heart and a choleric disposition. I had been regarding him for some time when I realised that he was not alone. A woman came forward and gripped his elbow in a familiar way, from which I deduced her to be his wife, and spoke some soft words to him, after which he patted her hand tenderly and announced that he was perfectly fine and that she was not to fuss. She nodded and returned beneath the tarpaulin that the master had hurriedly erected to protect us from the elements.

A foreign gentleman was also on the barge, a young man who did not, it seems, speak Dutch with any facility. It was no great intellectual achievement to identify him as a Pole or Lithuanian, no doubt on the first leg of a long journey home. At one point I exchanged a few words of Latin with him but, though civil, he was uncommunicative.

If only the same could have been said of Senguerdius, who, having exhausted his knowledge of the Peace of Westphalia, was now discoursing on the causes of inclement weather, pointing to defects in the ancient understanding which, he said, we might excuse as the inevitable concomitant of the Greeks living in a country that saw little rain. We Dutch are experts on precipitation of all kinds. It must be all the practice we get.

Darkness fell, but the master simply lit lanterns and hung them on the ends of the boat. [Van der Meer knows very well that I do not know what they are called; well, I do, actually, because they are the bow and the stern, but I am not absolutely sure which is which. He only asked me to satisfy his eccentric sense of humour by discomfiting me.] In this way we pressed on and finally arrived at our staging point at around two o'clock in the morning. Despite the hour, the innkeeper gave us a welcome, showing us to a newly swept corner of the floor where we might sleep; or, should I say, where we might have slept, had not the baker set about his business at four o'clock with a clanking of trays and a merry song or two to raise his spirits.

At six o'clock the innkeeper's daughter brought us a mug of warm beer and some freshly baked bread as a breakfast, and within the hour we were being marched the short distance to the river where our next barge would be waiting. Senguerdius secured the co-operation of a couple of local men to carry our trunks by ostentatiously drawing a gold coin from his pouch, returning it thereafter and paying them with some coppers instead.

The barge which was to take us along the Maas was an altogether grander affair. It had a sail which held out the prospect of a faster passage if the wind was in the right direction which, I was told, it was. There were also individual stools for the passengers so that we were not obliged to tolerate people leaning against us, and the enterprising master had a keg of ale from which he was prepared to supply us with drinks at a small charge.

The first part of the journey would take us to Roermond, and was expected to take us a day and most of the night. There we would rest before another journey of ten or twelve hours on to Maastricht.

The discovery that we were to pass through Roermond shook me a little. I had not realised that we were to travel through the heart of witch country. Of course, like any man of sense I did not believe in witches, but I could not help thinking that if I was mistaken about that Roermond was exactly the sort of place where they might lie in wait to prove me wrong.

CHAPTER FOUR

My first impression of Roermond was of a perfectly ordinary town with no evidence that the Lord of Darkness was at work there, except in the prices that we were charged for refreshments.

As a result of contrary winds and the need to row along the river it took longer than expected to reach Roermond and the bargemaster said that he would be glad of a rest, so we might have the remains of the day at leisure with a view to starting out for Maastricht at first light the next day.

One of the advantages of most Dutch towns is that they have walls around them, meaning that it is quite hard to get lost so long as you keep inside the gates. With much of the day to myself, and desiring to spend as little of it in the company of Senguerdius as I could manage, I declared my intention of hunting out a minister of religion to see if he knew of any good libraries. This was true, but my primary reason for announcing it was that I knew that Senguerdius had a particular disdain for provincial libraries and was planning to do some sightseeing instead. Thus informed, I knew that if I kept away from any landmarks I might well have the day to myself.

I had intended to put witches out of my mind, but a brief walk led me to a square where I found a plaque commemorating the burning of 75 people on or around that spot, and in no time I was assailed by a tinker who offered me a candle shaped like a witch tied to a stake which, he assured me, would effectively mimic the burning of a witch when lit. When I pointed out that witches are usually burned from the feet upwards rather than from the head down, he hurriedly put the wretched object away and attempted to interest me in a lucky rabbit's foot, to which I replied that since the rabbit had presumably had four of these but did not appear to have profited from them, I doubted their efficacy, at which the tinker used a filthy epithet and stalked away muttering about the clergy.

I found an inn and ordered a beaker of ale and a plate of bread and cheese. I was completely unprepared for the local cheese, which smelled foul, though it tasted better than its odour foretold. I washed it down with another beaker, handed over a few coppers in payment, and stepped outside again, only to be hailed by an all too familiar voice.

'Well met, Master Mercurius!' said Senguerdius. 'Have you enjoyed your day?'

'Thus far,' I said pointedly, though the nuance appeared to escape Senguerdius.

'Have you eaten?' he asked.

I jerked my thumb behind me. 'In there,' I said.

'Do you recommend it?'

'Not if you're a cheese lover.'

'Did they give you the smelly stuff?'

'I'm afraid so.'

'I've no idea how it happens but the cheese continues to ripen almost indefinitely,' Senguerdius mused. 'I must make a study of it one day. But enough of that.' He wrapped an arm around my shoulder again. I wished he would not do that. It was like being propositioned by a roué. 'I, on the other hand, found a bookstall with a little treasure on it.'

He gleefully produced a small dark red book for my inspection. I turned it to read the spine, but there was no title there, so I turned back the cover and flyleaf and read "A True

Account of the Recent Interrogation and Burning of many Witches in the town of Roermond".

'Do you expect to use this?' I asked.

'Of course! Not for the executions, obviously, but for the misinformation and papistical superstitions evidenced in the questioning.'

I considered briefly whether I needed to point out the dangers of using phrases like "papistical superstitions" before a jury with a majority of Catholics but decided that a man with two doctorates should be able to work that out for himself.

We began walking along the road together. I had not actually decided which way I was going, but Senguerdius seemed to assume I must be going the same way as him, and swept me along with him.

'I can sense your scepticism, Mercurius. You would do well to guard against such displays during the debate, but man to man I can allow that I cannot have explained matters to you in a sufficiently convincing fashion.'

I trawled my memory for any conversation that had touched upon any actual arguments Senguerdius proposed to deploy, assuming that scorn, sarcasm and vulgar abuse were discounted as tactics, but I could not recall such a discussion.

'Come, let us have a cup of wine in this superior establishment,' he cried, indicating a place to my left.

I wanted to ask how he knew it to be superior, since it looked very much like the one that I had just left, but I held my tongue; then it dawned on me that there were two well-dressed men sitting just inside the door sipping from goblets, so I suspect that he thought it must be a superior inn since it attracted a superior class of person as customers. I might have argued that some of the most unruly drunks I ever knew were men of rank. Did I need to remind Senguerdius of the recent incident when two merchants in Leiden got so drunk at a musical soirée that they peed in a lady's carriage, apparently mistaking it for the privy?

I found myself manoeuvred to a table, Senguerdius simultaneously guiding me into a chair and waving to the potboy to attract his attention.

'Now,' Senguerdius began in a low voice once our wine had arrived, 'it is time that I laid matters out in detail. We cannot leave anything to chance if you are to support me in the required way.'

I nodded. It was, I think, expected of me, though my hackles were, if not exactly rising, at least stirring themselves at the characterisation of our relative roles, Senguerdius as the main speaker and me as the light relief afterwards.

'As we agreed,' he continued, 'I shall speak first and you will tidy up afterwards, reinforcing my arguments and reminding the judges of the key points of our case.'

My recollection was that I had suggested that Senguerdius should go first but that we had not reached a firm conclusion. Apparently our tentative thoughts had firmed up during the journey.

'All the discussion is to be in Latin, except, where necessary, the questioning of witnesses…'

'Witnesses?' I interrupted.

'Yes, witnesses. Didn't I mention those, Mercurius? Well, each side can call experts to bolster their case, but it comes out of their time allocation.'

'And do we have any witnesses?'

'Of course not. If we employed other experts it would look as if we weren't experts ourselves. And it would weaken our case; what expert can testify that he has seen something not happen? Since the whole point of our argument is that witchcraft is imaginary it follows that no witness could say anything useful because they can't have seen anything to the point.'

'They might, perhaps, have uncovered some knavery masquerading as sorcery,' I objected.

'Ah, but then our opponents would simply say that is nothing to the point, because such people were only mimicking real witches and the fact that some are frauds does not mean that they all are. Faulty syllogism, you see, Mercurius. Major premise: some people are witches. Minor premise: some people are frauds. Faulty conclusion: witches are frauds.'

I will confess that at this point those hackles of mine began to elevate quite markedly. I needed no lessons in Aristotelian logic from Senguerdius or anyone else. I teach the stuff to undergraduates, and errors of the kind he had just described were a daily occurrence in my classes. Any premise of the type "Some X are Y" tells us virtually nothing about X, because it follows that some X are not Y. For example, some men are Dutch, and some men are Chinese. It does not follow that Dutchmen are Chinese.

Anyway, Senguerdius was still rattling on about the arrangements for the debate.

'Each speaker has eight hours, or, basically, one day, to make their point. It is agreed that if a speaker finishes speaking before their allotted time and two hours or more remain in the day, the next speaker will start, but I'm sure we will each use our eight hours to the full.'

He may have been sure. I wasn't. I could always read the longest Psalm to kill a bit of time but otherwise I had no idea what I would say. I had made some drafts and none of them had extended over as much as three hours. Perhaps I could propose a long lunch?

'Have you enough material to fill eight hours, Rector?'

'Of course. Haven't you?'

I could not look him in the eye, so I concentrated on the wine as I replied. 'I thought it prudent to leave some time to recapitulate your arguments,' I said, 'and I wasn't sure how long I would need for that.'

I can think of Rectors who would have seen through this flattery with no effort at all, but Senguerdius seemed to regard it as entirely right and proper.

'Very wise, if I may so, Mercurius. As soon as we arrive in Maastricht I shall give you an aide-memoire of the salient points, but you must guard it carefully. If those villains from Leuven discover that such a paper exists they're not above waylaying you in a dark corridor.'

'Surely they are clergymen?' I argued.

Senguerdius looked at me as if I were something he had stepped in. 'Yes, but they are Catholics, Mercurius. Some of them are likely to be Dominicans.'

He pronounced the word with the same distaste he might have displayed towards Satanists. I was not aware that Dominicans were disposed to attack men in alleyways, but I had to yield to Senguerdius' greater experience of debates. It was a shame he had selected me as his teammate, when there were plenty of other lecturers who would have been better debaters than me. My old friend Johannes Voet, for example, was a skilled lawyer, an upright man, and one with a prodigious ability to speak at length. If only Adriaan Heereboord had not drunk himself to death, he would have been ideal for the job. He loved an argument, which is just as well because he started plenty of them.

There was nothing to be gained by defending the reputation of Dominicans, so I simply nodded.

Senguerdius leaned forward like a schoolboy about to tell a dirty joke. 'I may say, Mercurius, that a large part of my argument will be based upon a careful analysis of past legal cases in which I shall, one case at a time, prove that the verdict was faulty.'

'That won't be much comfort to the women who were burned or hanged.'

'No,' Senguerdius conceded, 'but it may be some consolation to their families when they read the pamphlet containing my speech that will be published shortly after our great victory. For the greater honour of the University, of course; personal aggrandizement has no place in scholarly debate.'

'Perish the thought,' I said, then quickly checked that my tone had not offended him, but he seemed to have taken it at face value. 'A pamphlet is planned, then?'

'I have already made the arrangements. I haven't left space for your speech, I'm afraid; if I print yours I ought to print our opponents' too, and I see no reason to propagate their errors. I hope you understand.'

'Yes, Rector.'

'Excellent! I knew you were a man of sense.'

'Rector, how will the families of these poor women read your speech, since they may be illiterate?'

Literacy is very widespread in our country compared with some others. In England, for example, hardly anyone outside London can read except the clergy, and I have my doubts about some of them. Even so, the families of those ignorant country women were less likely to read well.

'A good question, Mercurius, and one to which I have not given sufficient thought. But I am sure that if I arrange for their local minister of religion to have a copy, I may rely upon him to read it from the pulpit. It will save him having to think up a sermon for a week at least.'

If it includes the whole of the eight hours it would suffice for a couple of months' sermons, I thought, but said nothing.

'Well, I'm glad we've had this little chat,' Senguerdius remarked as he drained his goblet. 'I'm going to do a bit more shopping. I must take my wife a little something.'

It would not have surprised me if he had gone back to buy another of those witch candles, but it transpired that he bought her a brooch. [Van der Meer has coughed to attract my attention. He wonders whether I ought to be more guarded in my comments about Senguerdius who is, after all, still alive. Indeed, he published a book only five or six years ago, *Rationis Atque Experientiae Connubium*, which I would translate as *The Marriage of Reason and Experience* and not, as one of my students thought, "Things to eat after enjoying a woman". I told Van der Meer that there was nothing in my text that I could not defend as true. Besides, Senguerdius can look after himself. And I'm six years older than him. I shall tell him to respect his elders.]

I watched him walk off and debated whether to have another cup of wine or not. I was still thinking when the innkeeper came to collect payment for the drinks, Senguerdius having left without settling the account.

I knelt in the cool of a church. One of the advantages of being doubly ordained is that I feel comfortable in any kind of church. The people who go there may differ, but it is the same God who inhabits these places.

I was deeply unhappy. I have had a blessed life, free from the daily struggles that so many others must contend with; there is always food on my table (if you can call it that after Albrecht has had his hands on it) and I have ample money for my needs. I have not lost a child, because I never had any, nor a wife, because I had none of them either, but if I have been solitary, I have never felt lonely. Well, I take that back; there were a few times in prison cells and such places, but that aside, I have been very content with my own company, particularly if I have a good book.

Sometimes people ask me what Heaven will be like. I do not know. But I think it must be more like Leiden and less like Paris or London. It will be a place of beautiful music praising God day and night; I will see some old friends and, no doubt, a few people I did not expect to see. My brother will be there, and my mother and grandmother, my father and one of my grandfathers. I am not sure about the other one. I never knew my other grandmother, so it will be pleasant to meet her. Women will rest from their drudgery, and men from their labours. And there will be the biggest library imaginable. That is where you will find me. If there is no library I am not sure how it could be called Heaven. I certainly wouldn't want to go there.

A fellow priest told me a story once. A Catholic died and went to Heaven. After a few days St Peter came to see him.

'How do you like Heaven?' he asked.

'It's very nice,' said the man.

'Good,' said St Peter. 'I'm glad you're settling in. Do you have any questions for me?'

'Yes,' said the man, 'there is one. I notice in a distant part of Heaven there is a section surrounded by a high wall. What is that?'

St Peter smiled. 'Oh,' he said, 'that's where we put the Calvinists. They think they're the only ones here.'

I smiled as I recalled the joke, earning myself a disapproving look from a woman who was dusting the benches. It must have been a Calvinist church.

CHAPTER FIVE

Still on my knees in the church, I was turning the accounts of the witch trials over in my mind, when I found my thoughts heading in an unexpected direction.

If I were about to be hanged or burned for a crime of which I was innocent, I would be making a fuss. As the guards dragged me to the pyre or the gallows, I would shout my innocence to anyone who might hear it. After all, writing a polite note is not going to make much difference at that stage. For that matter, all my noise won't either. But I am not going to an unjust death without letting everyone know that this was a monstrous miscarriage of justice. So why did those people condemned in 1613 go to their deaths so placidly? If Senguerdius and I were right, and there is no such thing as witchcraft, they cannot have been guilty.

I could think of three possible answers. Maybe the pamphleteers had lied, and actually the accused had screamed their innocence, but it had not been recorded, perhaps because such pamphlets customarily have to include an admission by the condemned that their punishment is just, in order to justify the acts of the authorities.

The second answer was that they really believed that they were guilty. This is not the same as being guilty, of course. People can be browbeaten into believing in their own wickedness. I had known a few poor individuals who had died by their own hands in the belief that they were not fit to live for some reason or other. This is where Catholics have a bit of a head start. Of course, Catholics are very good at feeling guilty. They are encouraged to do so from a young age. As a later convert I had escaped this indoctrination. But whatever we do, we know we can be forgiven through confession, penance and a spell in Purgatory. A lot of people think that Purgatory is the same as Hell, but that is not right. It may be as unpleasant, but the point of Purgatory is that it is somewhere you go to prepare you for Heaven. If you get to Purgatory you know that eventually you will be admitted to Paradise once your sins have been expiated. It functions rather like one of those benches in the hallways of great houses; if you are invited to sit there, you know you will eventually be seen. If the door is slammed in your face, you know you won't.

Protestants, on the other hand, are brought up to believe that God has already decided what will happen to each of us, and many think that Heaven has a fixed capacity so that only a proportion of us have any hope of entering that blessed place. Protestant or Catholic, if you are convinced that you are an evil person, you might welcome the flames as a means of improving your chances of God's acceptance. What happens to your body is unimportant compared with the ultimate fate of the soul.

Some worry that the act of burning the body prevents the resurrection of the dead, but in Paul's First Letter to the Corinthians he says that we will be raised with a new, spiritual body, so what happens to the old earthly one is completely immaterial. When I die and, please God, I am raised to Eternal Life, will it be as the middle-aged Mercurius in the story I now tell, or the old Mercurius who is dictating it? Neither; I will be some kind of Mercurius, but an improved kind. A man may marry a girl of seventeen and stay with her until she is eighty, when she will look very different, perhaps unrecognisable as the young girl, but he will see the same woman. What he sees is not the decaying body, but the Anna or Sara or Trijntje within.

There is something that is "Us" that remains constant despite changes to our outward appearance.

Anyway, it was possible that they had not objected because they thought they needed to suffer to assure themselves of salvation, and since unearned suffering is meritorious in the eyes of God, being innocent of the crime for which they were executed would be good for them.

The third possibility was in some ways the least appealing, and I owed it to my grandmother. I had forgotten the conversation until this moment, but she had shocked me some years before when we were discussing an execution we had heard about.

'Maybe she was just ready to go,' she said of the victim. 'If you're old and you have nobody to love you, or you think you're a burden to your children, and all that lies ahead of you is misery and slow starvation, or a long, lingering painful death due to a disease, you might think that half an hour of pain was worth it for a quick release.'

'Oma! That's tantamount to suicide, which is a sin!' I'd protested.

'It might be tantamount to it, but it isn't actually the same, is it? It's not suicide if someone else strings you up or heaves you on a fire, so it's not a sin, and you might still go to Heaven,' she maintained.

So perhaps at least some of the witches — maybe the old and lonely ones — were just happy to escape a life of poverty and toil. But that did not explain why the young ones, the mothers of small children, did not scream all the way to the flames.

An idea came to me, but I needed help to explore it. It was now 1686, and the great witch burnings in Roermond had taken place in 1613, seventy-three years ago. It was just possible that there were one or two old people in Roermond who had been witnesses of the event and could tell me whether the witches had really gone like lambs to the slaughter. Of course, they would have to be over eighty years old, but my grandmother had been past eighty when she died, so it was not impossible. But how would I find them?

The woman who had looked at me disapprovingly a few minutes before was still dusting anything inanimate in the church. This is, by the way, a basic activity of Dutch women. They make a fuss of anything living and they polish anything that isn't. I did not want to reveal the exact reason for my interest, because she might wonder why I was so interested in witchcraft, and Roermond was not a good place to exhibit a desire for such learning.

I removed my hat and bowed slightly. 'Madam,' I began, 'I am Master Mercurius of the University of Leiden, and I should be grateful if you could help me.'

'Alp yow?' she said.

I had forgotten that the locals spoke a strange dialect of their own, but by degrees I got her to understand my quest, assisted by my clerical clothing which afforded her some reassurance.

'I wonder if you know of any really old people nearby? People above eighty years of age.'

'Old people? There's Antje.'

'Antje?'

'She lives behind the Munsterstraat. You'll see an archway with the date 1655 over it. Go through there and ask someone to point out her cottage.'

Cottage was a rather grand description of her hut, but at least being small it was relatively easy to keep warm. Antje was wobbling around the house collecting a pan, water and an egg when I arrived.

'Come in, Dominie, come in!'

I was becoming more attuned to their patois by now. I introduced myself and was invited to sit on an old chest which doubled as a linen press, I think, while Antje sat on a stool by the stove.

'I do well, thank you, Dominie,' she said. 'The convent sisters are very kind. They don't have any rooms there at the minute but I'm on the list, they say.'

'Have you lived here long?'

'I don't know as I ever lived anywhere else, and that's the truth of it,' she declared. 'My mother told me I was born in that corner beside you, and when my father died I helped her here, and married my Jos, and we all lived here.'

I could not help thinking that a young married couple sharing a single room with the bride's mother was not ideal, but such is the lot of many of the poorer classes. The privacy I take for granted at the University is a very precious gift.

'Then Mother passed over, and it was just me and Jos. And the four children of course.'

'Four children?'

'Two survived, at least to adult age. Piet died eighteen months ago; past sixty he was. But Anneke is still alive, God be praised. She'll be sixty next spring, if she's spared.'

'If she's spared?'

'Winters here can be awful cruel. They carry a lot away, what with the rheum and the cough. But she's healthy now, and has two boys of her own who come to see their Oma every Sunday without fail, except when they don't.'

'I wonder whether you remember the witch trials many years ago?' I asked her.

'Oh yes! How could I forget? Such terrible things came out, you know. There were two women in this very street what was accused of congress with the Devil.'

'Congress? You mean...?'

'Yes. Bold as brass, they was. They said he had a long cold pizzle. Mind, it's my belief as they'd been in the woods eating them mushrooms that give you funny dreams. To my certain knowledge one of them was found to be a virgin when she was examined by the midwife, but they said that didn't prove that she didn't have congress because the Devil can have you magically without leaving any trace. In and out and you'd never know. Well, a God-fearing woman would, of course, if she was awake at the time.'

I was unsure whether this was getting me very far, but I decided to persevere.

'The accounts I've read all say that the condemned went to their deaths praying fervently, without protest, like lambs to the slaughter. Is that true?'

'No!' she drawled scornfully. 'Young Katja — her what was a virgin — she screamed loud enough to hear her in the town all the way to the Galgenberg.'

The Galgenberg was the little hillock outside town where they executed people, I discovered. It was cunningly situated on the south-east side of the town facing Germany so visitors from there would know what they were in for if they misbehaved, and there was a little chapel nearby.

'She protested her innocence?'

'She bit, kicked, yelled, tried to pull the balls off the sergeant, but that only annoyed him, and he smacked her round the face so hard they couldn't burn her for half an hour till she came round. It wouldn't be right to burn her unconscious, would it?'

If there was any logic to this last statement, I wasn't certain what it was, but I let it go.

'How old were you when this happened?' I enquired.

Antje pulled her mitts down so her fingers poked well out and appeared to be counting on them. 'I must have been eight or nine. Mother didn't want me to go, but neither did she want me left on my own because the witches were going around murdering children. Above six hundred of our newborns were killed, the magistrates said.'

I could not claim to have walked the whole of Roermond since we had arrived, but it was not as big as Leiden. Even if every house contained one woman of childbearing age, and every woman had a baby every eighteen months, that suggested that around a third or a quarter of all the children born in Roermond had been killed by witchcraft. I am no mathematician, and I accept that my numbers are estimates and cannot be supported with any certainty, but the sheer idiocy of these allegations must surely have been clear to everyone, mustn't it?

'Antje, did you personally know any children who were killed by witchcraft?'

She blinked as if she did not understand the question. 'You mean by name?'

'Their name or their family name.'

Again the old woman began reckoning on her fingers. I was beginning to dread the answer I was going to get when she finally spoke.

'No.'

'None at all?'

'Not personally. But I knew Jacob who lived at the riverside meadow and lost three cows.'

'Three cows?'

'Well, strictly, two cows and a heifer.'

'To witchcraft?'

'So they said. One was right as rain one minute, then bam! Over she went. Right on top of the heifer.'

I had never had the keeping of cows, but I was aware that sheep that were apparently very healthy sometimes just dropped dead, often after they had been sheared. Why should the same not happen to cows? [No, of course not after shearing, Van der Meer. Even I know you don't shear cows. I sometimes think the man says these things to provoke me. Maybe he's hoping I'll keel over one day and he'll inherit my money. I've half a mind to add a bit to my will instructing that my gold is to be fed to a bull, then Van der Meer can have the fun of following it around with a bucket and spade collecting his legacy as it reappears. Not that he knows that anything is coming to him. I'll remember him in my will though; it'll say "To my incompetent half-wit of a clerk, Jan van der Meer, I leave…" then whatever sum I come up with. I haven't decided yet. But I won't let him starve.]

The more I looked into this, the more convinced I was that the witch trials of 1613 were the result of hysteria. This was not to say that Antje was a silly old woman. She was perfectly average, but if enough average people think like that, then the result is mass delusion.

Around the time that I was born, this country succumbed to the tulip mania. People lost large sums of money paying ridiculous amounts for tulip bulbs. Obviously I have no first-hand knowledge of this, but if my information is correct, people were prepared to exchange entire smallholdings for a single bulb. Now, I draw the reader's attention to the key fact here; people lost a lot of money, therefore these were people who had money to lose. Since, in the general run of things, idiots do not get rich, we may assume that this hysteria was not the result of stupidity or even lack of education; and anyone who thinks that expensively schooled people do not believe strange things is cordially invited to sit in on one of my tutorials with undergraduates, where they will almost certainly hear propositions advanced that cannot survive the slightest scrutiny by an intelligent seven-year-old. Incidentally, I know quite a few intelligent seven-year-olds, but very few intelligent undergraduates. Something happens to them between these ages to dull their wits. They discover women, strong drink and lute music.

Be that as it may, my conversation with Antje had clarified some things for me. The chief discovery was that the pamphleteers' accounts could not be relied upon as accurate depictions of what had happened. Broadly, they reprinted gossip uncritically; and while this was helpful for exhibiting popular beliefs of the day, they brought us no nearer the truth. For example, one of the allegations against a witch was that she had caused four hundred women to miscarry their pregnancies, which might cause an unbiased investigator such as myself to wonder how. I don't mean the mechanism alone, though that defeats me, but as a proportion of all the women in Roermond it must have been quite incredible. Maybe there was not much to do in Roermond in the evenings, but it sounded as if every woman spent nearly her whole life pregnant. What motive could there possibly be for the witch in this? The usual response was that she hated all pregnant women, but why? How would she even know that a merchant's wife on the other side of town was pregnant, since such women rarely ventured abroad?

If I were to hear of such a catastrophe striking a town or village, I would think of some kind of plague. Perhaps the air is bad, or the water has become foul. I would not immediately think of witchcraft, but the notion that a witch is responsible is as pervasive and damaging as any plague.

I realised, somewhat belatedly, that Antje was sitting in front of me as these thoughts raced through my mind, and that it was impolite to ignore her.

'You said that Katja cried out as they led her to the flames. Were you there?'

'I was, Dominie. They burned two witches every day for a month or more, but I didn't go to them all. After all, I was only a child, and it was hardly fit for a young one to witness. I went just the once, with my mother.'

'Your mother took you to such a horrible event?'

'Just once. She wanted to go and she did not want to leave me unattended, so I went with her, though I spent much of the time with my face pressed into her skirts and my hands over my ears.'

'And that was when Katja suffered?'

'Yes.'

'Did you know her well?'

'I didn't know her at all, Dominie, but the other woman who was burned with her I knew very well. She was my mother's cousin.'

'A relative of yours was accused too?'

Antje shrugged. 'It's a small town and we're a bit out on a limb here. We marry local people, so it's very likely that we're all related to each other somehow or other. My husband's brother married my mother's niece, and my son married a niece of hers. You see how it is.'

This appalling thought had not struck me before. So many people died, in so small a community, that surely almost all of them would have been related to someone who suffered. They would have known that the allegations were untrue, and yet they did not rise up and oppose the magistrates. They allowed the collective madness to overcome their personal knowledge of the qualities of the victim.

Overwhelmingly those convicted were female. Now, I am not particularly knowledgeable about these things, but it seems to me that the world is run largely for the convenience and benefit of men. Put simply, men have a better life than any woman can. In almost every respect women are treated as inferiors and denied rights that men can freely exercise. So, I ask myself, if women have these terrifying occult powers, why haven't they used them to put men in their place? If I could turn someone into a toad, I would not waste that gift on any woman I can think of; rather, I would be settling scores with a number of men who have crossed me over the years.

I thanked Antje, and left her a little charity to ease her days, before slipping out into the relatively fresh air of the afternoon. It may have been my imagination, but everywhere I went I could smell burning.

I did not know what Senguerdius was going to say at this wretched debate, but I intended to hammer home the argument that if witches had the powers claimed for them, the world would be rather different. I owed that much to Katja.

CHAPTER SIX

The final leg of the journey to Maastricht was uneventful, largely because I spent much of it asleep. I am not a sunrise sort of person, so when we were roused before dawn so that the barge could have the full day to finish the trip I cannot say that I felt bright and chirpy to greet the day. Some of my working days begin at seven o'clock, which means that I have to rise before half past six in order to wash, shave and grab a little breakfast. Since I live next to my place of work I can soon be in place, which is more than some of my students can. To be fair to them, it cannot be easy to rouse yourself to hear a lecture on St Thomas Aquinas or Duns Scotus at seven o'clock when you were in a tavern until two o'clock.

As a student myself I was assiduous in my studies, largely because I knew what sacrifices my family had made to send me to Leiden and I did not want to have to face them if I did not make the most of them. When I graduated and was given the chance to stay at the University I worried what my mother would say, since she had been looking forward to my return home, but in the event she was so proud that I had been made a lecturer that I need not have worried. I am told that she managed to work my employment status into almost all her conversations for several months after my appointment. Our local minister told me once that they prayed every Sunday that I would be preserved from the temptations of the big city. Goodness, if they thought Leiden was a hotbed of sin I can only boggle at their reaction if they ever went to Amsterdam.

We tied up by the Grain Market and I surveyed the city. One of the advantages of looking for a church is that they dominate the skyline. In Maastricht's case there were a few churches in view. The nearest was the Roman Catholic Basilica of Our Dear Lady, where I would gladly have lingered, but Senguerdius had already marched resolutely on.

'Come along, Mercurius! I'm not paying these porters to stand watching you gawp at buildings!'

The red tower of St John's was next in view. I thought it was red stone, but as we got closer I could see that it was ordinary marl painted red to provide some protection against the rain.

Just behind St John's we came to the Basilica of St Servatius, where our unexpected arrival led to some confusion. I spotted some ecclesiastical types running away when we entered, which I thought inhospitable, until I realised that they were our counterparts from Leuven who did not think it proper to be the first people to greet us in Maastricht.

In no time a brother appeared, his arms folded inside the sleeves of his habit, and bowed slightly.

'Can I help you?' he asked, or something like that.

Senguerdius took charge. 'I am Wolferdus Senguerdius, Rector Magnificus of the University of Leiden...'

'Which God preserve,' I chipped in. I know my place.

'Indeed. And this is the celebrated Dr Mercurius, a leading light of the Faculty of Theology.'

I am still not used to being called "Doctor", and certainly I had never before heard any Rector call me a leading light of any part of the University, unless that's the same thing as being their "main embarrassment" or "our biggest waste of space". I did note, however, the use of the indefinite rather than the definite article, as if I were merely one of many leading lights.

'I am Brother Theodemar,' said our greeter. 'I will take you to our Prior and then your servants can carry your chests to your chambers.'

There followed a volley of local dialect which, I think, was to the effect that the porters were nobody's servants. Brother Theodemar mollified them by suggesting that if they took the chests to the building where the rooms were they could then have a beaker of ale while they awaited our return.

The church was a large one, but its main interest was in the crypt where there were numerous treasures and reliquaries. Bits of St Servatius' own skull were stored in a magnificent bust of him. I have no idea how they were found or what happened to the rest of his head.

In order to guard and manage these treasures a chapter of priests and other religious men had gathered to ensure that pilgrimages were conducted in a seemly, organised and extremely lucrative way. Say what you like about Catholic religious orders, they certainly know how to squeeze a man's purse.

One of their favourite tricks, which was in evidence that afternoon, was to close the crypt for a while. This meant that disappointed pilgrims had to stay in town until it was reopened and — wouldn't you know it? — the church just happened to have some guest rooms in which you could stay, and for a little extra meals could be provided. And no doubt you would have some dirty clothes after so long on the road, so you could have a bath while women did your laundry (at a price) and the same women would embroider a badge on your shirt so all your friends would know you had made the pilgrimage and possibly arrange for your shoes to be repaired before your return journey, which, of course, would not be until after Mass on the following Sunday when you could see a procession of relics (good places near the front to be booked at a very reasonable rate) and maybe buy a souvenir or two.

The poor chapter had suffered a grievous blow in 1632 when the city was captured by our Dutch forces and hence separated from the Spanish empire. This brought to the end the Pilgrimage of the Relics, when tens of thousands came on a tour of holy places every seven years. The pilgrims still came to nearby Aachen but did not dare cross the border into a country which was nominally Protestant, so the income of the chapter had declined for a while, until they were able to think up some new money-making schemes.

They had been only too willing to host the debate. Not only would they expect generous donations from the two universities, but it gave them an excuse to close the buildings for the week, which meant the pilgrims would be at their mercy for a while. I was unsure whether to be more offended by the witch candles in Roermond or the piece of St Servatius' finger bone that I was offered by one of the porters. The light was not good and he seemed reluctant to let me take it towards a window, but I saw enough to know that St Servatius must have been one of our most remarkable saints, being part chicken.

We were shown to our rooms, which were commendably spartan. On the assumption that everyone else's was much the same as mine, they each contained a wooden bed with a straw mattress laid over the slats, a woollen blanket, a bolster pillow, probably stuffed with horsehair, a small stand on which a pitcher and bowl stood, and a prie-dieu where we could say our prayers. A crucifix normally stood over the head of the bed but had been tactfully removed for the Reformed team, leaving a paler outline on the wall where it had previously hung. My chest was placed at the foot of the bed, so when the porters had gone I moved the bolster to the other end which allowed me to put my book on the chest without having to get out of bed. I then realised I did not have a candle in the room, so I could not read anyway.

I had naturally assumed that everyone's room was the same, but of course the judges were much better provided for. As if a bishop — even an auxiliary one — would sleep on a straw mattress! Johann Heinrich von Anethan turned out to be much less vain than many a prelate I have known — indeed, he was austere, as bishops go — but there are limits.

It transpired that von Anethan had arrived in the city, but was paying a courtesy visit to someone important and would not reach the church until the morning. There would be two simultaneous church services at eight o'clock, one for the Catholics and one for the Reformed (which essentially meant Senguerdius and myself, since the two Protestant judges had not arrived) before the debate began at ten o'clock.

When I say "the debate began" I mean, of course, interminable speeches of welcome from the Prior, the local church dignitaries, the Mayors of Maastricht, the leader of each team and anyone else they could think of who wanted to say a few words before we all sat down to a celebration dinner, so no actual debating would be done on the first day. This was something of a relief to me, because I had seen no sign of Senguerdius writing any notes. I admit that he had been leafing through a book, but when I taxed him about his apparent lack of preparation he was quite caustic.

'It is a capital error to over-rehearse, Mercurius. One loses the freshness. The phrases become hackneyed and stale. And there is always the temptation to embellish one's sentences and thereby lose their crystalline purity.'

Did he actually believe this stuff? Who knows? He was sufficiently brilliant to beat many a man by relying on his own wits, but he was up against men of a similar stamp. As I dictate this, nearly forty years later, I must allow that the University at Leuven was not at its apogee then. A number of notable professors had died, and if the debate had been thirty years earlier I think we would have faced a much greater challenge.

This is a good point at which to introduce the Leuven team. The junior member was Zeger Bernhard van Espen, who was younger than I was, but already a noted authority on canon law (as, indeed, he still is as I write). Van Espen was junior in rank, but Leuven had opted to have him speak first for them. This was good for me, because it invited the judges to compare him with Senguerdius rather than with me. Since I was by no means confident that I could outshine Van Espen, this suited me very well.

Incidentally, had we known the exact terms of Van Espen's contract with the University of Leuven I believe that Senguerdius might have objected to his participation, because although nominally a professor, Van Espen was obliged to teach only six times a year, and even these were during the long vacation in the summer. When I discovered this I felt a few pangs of jealousy, since the prospect of only having to teach undergraduates after most of them had gone home appealed to me very much, until I recollected that those who remained were probably there to cram for resit examinations having failed the first time around; and when you look at the calibre of those who scrape a pass you soon realise that those who fail must be quite astonishingly dim-witted. Even six lectures a year might tax a man's patience. In my young days I knew a farmer who talked to his oxen, it being his belief that they would be more compliant if he had given them a full explanation of what he wanted them to do. In the event they did what they wanted to do, regardless of his wishes, showing no understanding at all of his explanation and merely regarding him with big, sad brown eyes as he attempted to drum it into them. I rather fancy Van Espen would have understood the farmer's struggles by the end of each summer.

The other member of the Leuven team was the Rector Magnificus, Petrus Govarts. Govarts was no less brilliant than Senguerdius, having a doctorate in law, and being a professor of both rhetoric and philosophy. When I discovered that he was six years younger than me I could have spat. Govarts is currently Vicar Apostolic at 's-Hertogenbosch, though he was prohibited from entering the place for some reason. Personally I can think of no better outcome for a churchman than to be paid to do a job that the civil authorities then stop you doing, and I would accept the position at once and then head for the nearest library, but as I understand it Govarts spent six years arguing that he should be allowed back and finally paid a large fine to settle the matter.

A brother knocked on the door to announce that vespers would begin in ten minutes, after which we would take a simple supper. I took it from this that we were expected to attend the church service. There is a requirement that priests should say vespers each day, and I do, usually, most of the time, if I am not busy, but I do not understand why people assume that clerics are itching to get to church at every opportunity. Anyway, I obediently followed him to the chapel. Since vespers is not a sacrament there is no barrier to a Reformed person joining in the prayers, so it was no surprise to find Senguerdius there. What was a surprise was that he made a point of not kneeling for some parts of the service just to emphasise that he was not a Catholic, so I felt I had to do the same. The reader will understand how uncomfortable this was for me.

Vespers being concluded, we filed into a refectory to share a simple supper. I am bound to say that if this was representative of their normal repasts the chapter at St Servatius did themselves very well. A bowl of broth formed the first course, and was easily identifiable as ham and barley. I shudder to think what Albrecht could have done with such ingredients. We then had roast pork with turnips and peas, and there was an apple for each of us after that. I do not have a large appetite, but I think I can claim that Leiden acquitted itself well at the table that evening. Senguerdius chatted happily with anyone who would listen, whereas I contented myself with a few words and a lot of chewing. Fortunately I was sitting opposite Van Espen, who did not seem disposed to talk much and rather resented the meal as keeping him from writing another brilliant treatise that evening. As soon as the platters were cleared he bowed politely and returned to his room.

'Come, Mercurius,' said Senguerdius as we rose from our benches, 'let us take a quick look at the scene of our coming triumph,' and led the way to the Emperor's Hall. It was quite magnificent, with large stone arches and wonderful acoustics, perhaps as a result of a fairly low roof. Chairs had been laid out for the guests. There were five on the dais, one for von Anethan as chief judge and the others for the four debaters. Each team had a table in front of them to store notes and books.

Facing us were six chairs in a row for the panel, and an extra one at each end for the two mayors of Maastricht. For reasons which escape me now, the city had a Catholic mayor (Johannes Emericx) and a Protestant one (Servaes van Panhuysen).

There was also a lectern at one side where any expert witness who might be called would stand. I knew that we had none, and I had seen no sign of one called by Leuven, but provision had been made anyway.

The room was well furnished with candles and I could not fault the arrangements that had been made.

'Early night for us, eh, Mercurius?' Senguerdius boomed, slapping me on the back. 'No carousing this evening!'

As if I ever caroused.

Anyway, I wanted to have another read through my notes, which is what I must have been doing when I fell asleep and only woke as the bell struck four o'clock, by which time I had a painful crick in my neck.

The morning service passed uneventfully, as did breakfast, and at a few minutes to ten o'clock we filed into the Emperor's Hall for the formal opening. The judges had all arrived, it seemed, but had dined separately so as to avoid any risk of being suborned by the debaters. Needless to say, the thought of nobbling a judge would never have occurred to me, and I chose to think that Senguerdius would feel the same way.

Von Anethan spoke first, and I was pleased to hear that he addressed us in Latin, which is my preferred language for scholarly activity. No doubt I could manage in Dutch, though some phrases would have to be constructed to convey the whole of the meaning, but if the Leuven professors had spoken in the Flemish dialect I might have been troubled. Everyone says that Flemish and Dutch are mutually intelligible, which they are, once your ear adapts, but I should have spent too much time mentally correcting their pronunciation, as I was already doing with the Maastricht residents.

We were formally greeted by the Prior, who drew our attention to the many opportunities the church afforded us to spend money, and who expressed the hope that our rooms would be serviceable without ever crossing the line into "comfortable". I think we can safely say that goal was achieved. He introduced some of the other brethren, including Theodemar, who bowed meekly at the mention of his name, and Gerlach, the hospitaller. I mention him particularly because he will play a part in our tale in a short while, so I beg the reader will remember him.

While Theodemar had supervision of the guesthouses, Gerlach looked after the sick and had some medical knowledge. In fact, I will go so far as to say that in learning he was the equal of most physicians, and in kindness and charity he was much their superior. Of course, they worked hand in hand, Gerlach encouraging weary and footsore pilgrims to rest a while, and Theodemar promptly appearing with a list of the services that could be had there, carefully keeping his thumb over the prices as he pointed to each in turn.

The mayors each addressed us in the local dialect, so I have little idea what they said or even which was which, but their speeches were mercifully brief, partly because neither really wanted to be there and they left at the earliest opportunity, when von Anethan had introduced the judges and reiterated the rules of the contest.

As the proposers of the motion, Leuven would speak first, in the person of Van Espen. After his eight hours, probably on the second day, Senguerdius would reply for us. Govarts would then be the third speaker, and I would be the last, after which Senguerdius could summarise for up to an hour, followed by Van Espen doing the same for Leuven. The judges would then retire to consider their verdicts, each in turn speaking in an order drawn by lot, with von Anethan bringing up the rear. He thought that no more than two days would be required for this, which shocked me. I had expected that it could be done by a show of hands, but apparently each would deliver a consideration of all the evidence before declaring their judgement. It was likely that we would be here for the entire week.

I grant that a whole seven dinners away from Albrecht's culinary immolations would be welcome, but I was already pining for a good library. If there was one at St Servatius' I had not yet tracked it down.

I was feeling sorry for myself when I suddenly realised that von Anethan must have stopped talking because everyone was getting up and heading for the door. Senguerdius was so busy chatting to Govarts that he had not bothered to alert me to the move, so I hastened to follow because I had no idea where we were going next.

It transpired that we were being entertained to dinner by the mayors. It did not seem that long since breakfast, and to make matters worse as I rushed along the corridor my eye caught a glimpse of something tempting in a side chamber.

A room full of books.

CHAPTER SEVEN

Books! Books are my friends, my most engaging company, my boon companions. I love the feel of a well-bound book, its tight spine, its crisp pages. They smell so seductive, at least when they are new. Like mature women, they retain their fascination well into middle age if they be well cared for and kept free from dust and mould (books, that is — not women — I have never come across a mouldy woman).

You can imagine my feelings, therefore, when I was obliged to leave a whole room of them unexamined in order to have dinner with the mayors. I am not a gourmet, or even a gourmand. I live a sedentary life and therefore do not need much food to keep me going, nor am I so gregarious as to enjoy the experience of eating with strangers. The shy ones do not speak to me, and I am unlikely to speak to them, being of a reserved temperament [Marginal note: Van der Meer appears to have a nasty, if very selective, cough at present] and the outgoing ones monopolise the conversation so I cannot get a word in. Either way, communal eating is a trial to me.

On this occasion, however, I found myself sitting opposite Abbess Mathilde. Women are naturally more communicative than men, but are also good listeners (perhaps so that they do not miss any gossip) and this made for a much more enjoyable experience. Senguerdius and I had been separated, but some thought must have gone into the seating, because Van Espen and Govarts were also distant from each other but also from us. On my left side I had the Protestant mayor, Servaes van Panhuysen, and on the right was a fellow called Friedrich Armand, who was very taciturn, partly because he spoke only

German. Maastricht being so close to Germany, those from that city were able to converse with him, so I left him to speak to Theodemar on his right side and concentrated all my attention on Abbess Mathilde.

Mathilde was a striking woman, tall and slender of form, and like most nuns she had wonderfully clear skin. Whether this is due to sanctity or the avoidance of any cosmetic artifice I cannot say, but I have rarely met a nun with a poor complexion. She spoke quietly and her face when reposed had a gentle smile upon it, which was very pleasing. She seemed to be a woman of great contentment of heart, though I noticed her giving a sharp look to a servant who overlooked her until the men had been served.

'I am afraid the potboy thinks you will not drink wine,' I said, as much to deflect any anger that might cloud her face, and signalled to him to return to his duty.

'Thank you, Dr Mercurius,' she said, betraying a magnificent deep yet feminine voice. I should have loved to hear her sing the Psalms in that contralto tone. 'Though I think he probably thought to attend to the men first, don't you?'

'I fear so,' I mumbled, as if I were the derelict one, and resolved to exhibit only the finest table manners in her presence. To be honest, she frightened me a little. It was plain that she did not suffer fools gladly — or, possibly, at all.

In order to keep the peace, I leant to my left to murmur to Van Panhuysen, who summoned the servant and instructed him quietly to see that the lady was served immediately after von Anethan, who was to her right.

Before attacking my food, I paused to say grace. Since we were not of one faith, we had been invited each to say it privately in our preferred form, which I did, and was surprised to see Abbess Mathilde smiling at me as I raised my head after doing so.

'Not quite as Protestant as you would have us believe, Dr Mercurius?' she said quietly.

I had thought I was praying silently, but I have an occasional fault of voicing my thoughts unconsciously, which I must have done here, unless she was a practised lip-reader. I have known a few deaf people who could tell what you had said by watching the movements of your mouth, though I have no skill in that direction myself. Once, when I was ten or so, I saw my father across the field say something when the ox stood on his foot, but that owed more to my certainty of the kind of thing that Father would say in those circumstances rather than a close examination of his lips.

The meal was better than I had expected in such a place. For a start, none of it was burnt, which gave it a head start over the University of Leiden's refectory. I ate some of the fish as I usually do, choosing to eat it when I can to compensate for those Fridays when I cannot have it, and there were plenty of vegetables, including leeks and endives, onions and turnips. Mathilde restricted herself to these and a little bread. I offered her the platter of cheese, but she declined politely, explaining that she had eaten sufficient and feared that the cheese might be too rich for her on top of the vegetables. That thought had not occurred to me, but finding that one of the cheeses was the local stinky version I pushed the platter away. Armand felt no such compunction, and cut himself a large wedge of it, tearing a piece of the loaf to accompany it. I noticed that he was helping himself liberally to the jugs of beer while engaged in occasional conversation with Theodemar, who seemed to be competent in German, though Armand was doing most of the talking.

There is a fine line between making polite conversation and being downright nosy, and I may have trodden close to the line in asking Mathilde about her convent and the sisters there, but I thought these were safe topics.

It was at this point that Mathilde surprised me considerably.

'I have read your monograph against Socinus,' she said.

This placed her firmly in a very small number of scholars. I haven't even read it myself for some years.

'Your case against Socinus is convincing,' she said, 'but you seem rather grudging in your support of Abelard, I think.'

Suddenly I was returned to my student days, when an astute professor spots a hole in your argument and pins you through it. She was absolutely right, of course. I have never liked Abelard as a person, and this may have coloured my reflection on his work. Naturally I have some sympathy for any man forcibly castrated by order of his girlfriend's uncle, but in my view he was something of a narcissist, insufficiently humble, and somewhat more dogmatic than is fitting. However, when it came to theories of the atonement, I had to admit I preferred his ideas to those of either Anselm or Socinus.

[Marginal note: Van der Meer says I can't leave it there or readers will be puzzled. I doubt most readers care much one way or the other, but for the benefit of the few; the atonement refers to the idea that Jesus Christ died to pay for our sins, and Anselm suggested that this was a payment in satisfaction of a debt, which seemed to me to place the Devil on a par with Almighty God, as if God could not obliterate the debt in any other way; Abelard preferred to say that Jesus' death was an act of supreme love for us, whereas the wretched Socinus had proposed that Jesus died to set a moral example of dedication and self-sacrifice for us all, as if mere men were capable of emulating him. Needless to say, this is a very abbreviated version of my monograph, which ran to around twelve pages. Or was it fifteen? I must find my copy and read it again.]

'I accept the rebuke,' I said meekly. 'You are right.'

Mathilde appeared shocked. 'A man who accepts a woman's opinion! And they say that there are no miracles nowadays.'

I could not think what to say, then I noticed that she was smiling again, and I just smiled wryly back.

When dinner was ended, I asked Theodemar if I might browse the library.

'I'd like that too, if I may,' said Mathilde.

Theodemar looked at her as if the idea that a woman might be able to read had not previously occurred to him, but recovered himself sufficiently to agree to conduct us there.

'I hope you will stay,' Mathilde said, 'for the sake of appearances.'

'I assure you,' I began, 'that I would never think…'

'I meant only that a judge ought not to be alone with a disputant,' Mathilde explained.

'Ah, yes, of course,' I stuttered.

'I never anticipated any impropriety,' she continued, 'for I am protected by my Holy Cloth and your unimpeachable conscience.'

I am not that sure that my conscience was entirely unimpeachable at that moment, though it goes without saying that a priest must be very careful in his dealings with women, particularly when they are nuns. I suspect that my bishop's response to any impiety of that sort would have been very similar to that of Abelard's girlfriend's uncle. And then there would be the prospect of a very unpleasant interview at God's judgment seat in due course. There is a special corner of Hell reserved for priests who mess about with nuns, and I don't want to go there.

Theodemar led us to the cave of wonders and waited patiently while we goggled at the shelves. There were books there whose existence I had never suspected, others believed to be lost, and some that I had long wanted to read. But I was only to be here for a week! Perhaps I might make some arrangement to return someday, I thought.

Mathilde stepped daintily upon a stool to inspect the top shelf. 'Look, Dr Mercurius! Such delights!'

She read some titles to me and was plainly as enraptured as I was by this treasure trove.

'Brother Theodemar,' she exclaimed, 'I am surprised that this room is not kept locked. Do you not worry that such priceless volumes may be stolen?'

'In normal times, Abbess, the library is locked whenever the outer doors of the building are open, and may only be consulted after Vespers, though of course books may be borrowed by the community. The unlocking was by order of the Prior in honour of our guests.'

One did not need to possess supernatural powers of divination to grasp that Theodemar had considered the instruction to be a mark of the utmost folly.

'I trust the same concession has not been extended to the treasury,' Mathilde remarked.

'Indeed not! Nor, I regret, do I have present access to the key. The Prior himself is holding it.'

'Isn't that inconvenient when you celebrate the Mass?' I asked.

Theodemar turned his eyes away as if the answer made him uncomfortable.

'It is not so in normal times, when I can use the key. But when strangers are in the precincts, the Prior thought it prudent … not that he has any unworthy suspicions of any judges or participants!' he hastily added.

'I would not blame him if he did,' Mathilde answered. 'I can only speak for my own conscience and have never met any of the others before.'

'There are people here now whom we would not ordinarily receive,' Theodemar explained. 'Delivery boys from fish and flesh merchants, for example.'

'Unlikely to be tempted by books, but they will know the value of silver,' Mathilde smiled.

'And gold! We have some very fine golden vessels.'

'Then I am sure that prudence is the best course,' Mathilde continued.

I moved nearer the stool. Mathilde was turning back and forth to speak and I feared that she might fall, in which event I hoped that I would have the wit to catch the woman rather than follow my natural inclination to save the book.

She did not fall, of course. Swivelling first on one foot, then the other, she stretched to each side as sure-footed as any gymnast, at one point reaching so far that she gave us an inadvertent glimpse of her ankle, a fact conveyed to me by the violent reddening of Theodemar's face and his hurried turn of his head. Naturally I followed his previous gaze and then followed suit. Theodemar showed such confusion at the sight that I fell to wondering how he supposed women's legs were connected to their feet if not by ankles, but that was probably unkind. I suppose that he had never had to pick Fat Lysbeth off the cobbles outside Steen's Inn and prop her inside the door when she had taken too much of "something to keep the cold out". There were few parts of Fat Lysbeth that had not been exposed to public view at some time or another, especially if business was slack. As she used to say, with her you got a lot more whore for your money.

However, I digress. I hasten to explain that I am not making any comparison between Fat Lysbeth and the Abbess Mathilde. Indeed, Lysbeth was an honest woman in her own way, making no bones about how she earned her living, her necessity to do so and that in her view she was no different from wives who submitted to their husband's embraces not out of love but in the hope of a new dress or a jewel. I needed to shake my mind out of this line of thought before curiosity got the better of me and I inadvertently asked the Abbess for her thoughts on these matters.

Mathilde climbed down from the stool with a graceful little hop.

'Forgive me, Theodemar! I am being selfish, keeping you here when no doubt you have duties to attend to. Dr Mercurius and I must allow you to go about your work.'

I would have been very content for him to lock up, even with me still inside. Leave me with a jug of ale, some bread and a chamber pot and you could have bricked the entrance up so far as I was concerned, but I could see the fairness of her point.

'Of course,' I replied. 'Theodemar, I mustn't allow my enthusiasm for your library to disrupt your day.'

I hoped he did not detect my gritted teeth through which I spoke.

'The outer doors are locked, so there is no need for me to lock the library,' Theodemar answered. 'Are you sure that you can find wherever you want to go?'

'I must return to my chamber,' Mathilde replied. 'I should read and pray for an hour or two.'

'I must do the same,' I blurted out. Seeing the look on Theodemar's face I quickly added, 'Not to your chamber, of course. I meant my own. Alone. Obviously.'

Mathilde smiled that gentle smile of hers again. 'I think we knew that, Dr Mercurius.'

I hate wasting time; by which, of course, I mean that I hate wasting time when I am not the one deciding how my time is wasted.

I wanted to announce that we all knew how this was going to end. Whatever was said, everyone was going to vote the way they had already decided, and we were going to lose, despite Senguerdius' cunning jiggery-pokery with the selection of judges, so we might as well buy our souvenirs and get back to our proper jobs

There were some fine gardens around the St Servatius Church so I took a small book from my store and went for a stroll, reading as I went. I was gratified to catch a glimpse of Senguerdius at a window with his head down over some books, apparently finally succumbing to the need to do some homework. While I watched he flicked from book to book, scribbling a few lines from time to time though his handwriting was fairly grotesque at the best of times, so how he hoped to read notes made in haste I could not tell.

As I walked past one of the lower windows I could see a candle inside through stained glass and heard a female voice singing. It must be Abbess Mathilde, I thought. Listening intently, I picked out some of the words of Psalm 31: *Delictum meum cognitum tibi feci, et injustitiam meam non abscondi. Dixi: Confitebor adversum me injustitiam meam Domino; et tu remisisti impietatem peccati mei.*

Which is to say: Then I acknowledged my sin to you, and I did not hide my misdoing; I said, 'I will confess my misdoings to the Lord', and you remitted the guilt of my sin.

I found it very hard to imagine that the Abbess had any sins to confess to the Almighty. I, on the other hand, was in sore need of Confession of my sins, which were racking up by the minute. I am not admitting to carnal thoughts, you understand; nothing was further from my mind. Well, further from the front of my mind, anyway. I simply wanted to spend my days in her company. I would not lay a finger on her (though that would be a terrible waste) but would just bask in having found a female mind that permitted a conversation of equals on serious matters.

I was so engrossed in these thoughts that I completely failed to notice a tiny box hedge edging the path, tripped over it, and fell face first into some rose bushes.

Vanity being a sin, there were no looking glasses in the church buildings, so I had no opportunity to inspect my appearance after I had rushed to wash the dirt off, but I could tell by the reaction of those I passed in the corridors that I must have presented quite a sight. Nobody said anything, of course. In the Low Countries people do not interfere with the pleasures of others, and no doubt they thought that if I chose to mortify the flesh by diving headfirst into rose bushes I must have my reasons for doing so.

The first person to make any comment on my state was Theodemar, who seemed quite shocked. 'Have you been attacked, Master?' he asked.

'Attacked?'

'There is a tomcat who likes to sleep on the kitchen windowsill and lashes out at those who try to dislodge him.'

'No, it's not that. I'm afraid I fell over outside.'

'Let me conduct you to see Gerlach for some salve, and while he attends to you the laundrywomen can brush your gown.'

'That would be very kind,' I said. 'Thank you.'

CHAPTER EIGHT

Theodemar led me to a small hut where Gerlach was at work mashing some herbs in a mortar. He attempted to stand when I entered but since he was a tall man and the hut was very small he succeeded only in banging his own head.

'Please sit here, Master, and I'll fetch a soothing ointment. But first we must check that no thorns are left in your skin to fester and I must clean your skin with some wine.'

Cleaning wounds with wine is a time-honoured practice, but usually practitioners use the wine that nobody would want to drink. Gerlach's flask smelled divine.

'I dissolve a little incense in it,' he explained. 'It seems to work better that way.'

He held a lamp close to my face, so close that I felt uncomfortable with its heat so near, but it allowed him to find several small pieces of grit or thorn and remove them with tweezers before rubbing my skin with his wine. It stung a little as he dabbed the cuts and scratches, suggesting that I was more marked than I had thought, and he paid special attention to an area by my left eyebrow.

'There's a bit of a swelling there. Let's deal with that first.'

He left without any explanation and returned with a small piece of ice that must have come from a cold store somewhere. Wrapping it in a piece of linen he pressed it against my head.

'You're not feeling dizzy? About to faint?'

I assured him that I was not. The only time I have ever come near to fainting in such circumstances was when I needed to see a physician about a nasty cough. It wasn't the treatment. I just had a funny turn when he gave me the bill.

Gerlach stood for some minutes with the ice against my head, then suggested that I might hold it myself while he attended to the other scratches. He gently applied an ointment to my face and smoothed it with the most delicate of touches.

'That should do it, Master. If you need some more please come back. I'll seek you out before Vespers to see how that lump is.'

I thanked him for his kindness and automatically fished in my pouch for some coins.

'There's no charge, Master,' he said. 'I don't even have an alms box in here.'

He must have been the only man there who hadn't.

I headed for my room, in which I was so unsuccessful that I found myself in the large square outside and had to ask a local the best route to the guesthouse. She immediately crossed herself and ran away while others turned their heads as if I had the evil eye.

The only man who seemed unconcerned was a poorly-dressed fellow who was singing quietly to himself while swigging from a wineskin.

'Ho! Green man!' he called to me.

'Green?'

'Your face is green,' he insisted, 'though your hands are like ordinary men's.'

'That's just some ointment,' I said, once the reason had dawned on me.

'You got leprosy then?' he asked.

'No.'

'Well, you would say that, wouldn't you, on account of a leper what escaped would be strung up.'

'I assure you that I don't have leprosy or any other serious disease.'

'You're wearing lepers' rags.'

'My gown is being laundered. They lent me this one. It's quite old, I think.'

He appeared unconvinced, belched loudly and took another swig. 'Maybe it's my public duty to send for the watch to have a dangerous leper arrested.'

'I'm not a leper.'

'How much is it worth to you for me not to call the watch then?'

'I beg your pardon?'

'How much will you give me if I don't call the watch?'

I ask the reader to reflect that I taught ethics from time to time, and this kind of argumentation riles me. Ethics are not contingent on money changing hands. Either something is the right thing to do, and we should do it, or it is not, and we shouldn't. I started to explain this but then recalled that I was attempting to teach ethics to a drunk in a public place and gave up. It is hard enough to get undergraduates to take the core principles of ethics on board, and they are sober; well, some of them, anyway.

'If you feel you ought to call the watch, please do so.'

He giggled. 'Nah, you're all right, Green Man. I'm not on duty today.'

I secluded myself in my room in the hope that the salve would work quickly, and a couple of hours later there was a knock at the door and a pretty young girl entered with my folded gown in her arms. She said something or other in the local dialect, bobbed, and looked around for somewhere to put it down, finally settling on placing it across the bed. I had it in mind to give her a tip for her work, but when I stood up and turned fully towards her she gulped, bobbed once more and ran out of the door. If it had been open, that might have worked; as it was, she thudded into the oak and dropped like a shot duck.

I would have gone for help, but I couldn't open the door without moving her, so I picked her up and laid her on the bed, carefully moving my newly laundered robe so she did not crease it. I remembered what Gerlach had done for me, but I had no ice. On the other hand, my jug contained some cold water from the morning, so I found a kerchief and soaked it in cold water, commencing to hold it against her bruised nose. Thankfully, after a few moments she opened her eyes slowly as I sat beside her with a cloth over her nose.

Goodness, for a small girl she could scream.

Soon the doorway was jammed with people. Where were they all when I fell over in the garden?

Theodemar pushed his way to the front. 'What happened here?' he demanded of the girl.

'I don't know,' she said. 'I came to deliver the gentleman's cloak, then I woke up on the bed.'

The collected eyes of the crowd turned to me. I knew what they were thinking.

'She walked into the door,' I explained. 'I had to move her to get out.'

'Why would she walk into a door?' someone asked.

Fortunately, at this point something came back to her.

'He made me jump. I was frightened.'

'Frightened? Why, child?'

I recognised the calm, sensible voice of the Abbess who must just have arrived.

'Well, his face, ma'am. He's not normal.'

'I can see why you thought that. But I can assure you that he is just like you and me. Now, shall we be tranquil and ask why Dr Mercurius has painted his face green?'

'I didn't,' I protested. 'I fell and Gerlach treated my cut face with a salve. I didn't know it was coloured.'

'There you are,' said Mathilde. 'A perfectly sensible answer. How do you feel now?'

I opened my mouth to speak, then realised that she was asking the girl.

'Better, thank you, ma'am.'

Mathilde whispered something in the girl's ear, which appeared to shock the young woman. She felt her own lower stomach with her hand and whispered something back, at which the Abbess smiled and squeezed her hand gently.

'No harm done then,' Mathilde announced. 'If you're quite recovered they're probably missing you in the laundry.'

The girl took the hint, sprang off the bed and curtseyed to Mathilde, then me, before waiting for the crowd to move so she could get out of the room. Soon we were alone, although Theodemar waited in the doorway.

'I am glad that the girl was merely over-excited,' Mathilde said, and stood to leave.

'Thank you,' I stammered. 'I would hate people to think that I…' I could not find the words to finish the sentence.

'So would I,' Mathilde answered, 'especially since their unworthy thoughts would have been utterly wrong.'

She sailed out of the room like a majestic ship in full sail, acknowledging Theodemar who grasped the door handle.

'Shall I close this for you?' he asked.

'If you please,' I said and, when he had done so, I flopped back on the bed.

I realise that there are many people in this world who do not have enough to eat, some of them in my own homeland, so I do not wish to appear callous or ungrateful when I say that I sighed at the discovery that we were being summoned to another meal.

This was an informal supper, and the only thing that made me partake of it was the knowledge that it would be ten or eleven hours before we had anything else to eat. I took some bread and a bowl of broth and sat at one corner of the table in an attempt to reduce the number of people who might attempt to converse with me. This stratagem failed utterly because Senguerdius spotted me there and decided to initiate a discussion about tactics.

'You will be pleased to hear, Mercurius, that I have made significant discoveries today. Our case, which was already strong, is now unassailable.'

'I am delighted to hear it,' I said, while mentally substituting the word "astonished" for "delighted". His confidence, while admirable in many circumstances, chilled my blood. I could not help but recall Proverbs 16:18, *Contritionem praecedit superbia, et ante ruinam exaltatur spiritus*, which may be translated as "pride goes before destruction and a haughty spirit before a fall".

I began to worry that he could read my thoughts because he was staring fixedly at me, but he soon dispelled that idea.

'You will pardon my curiosity, I'm sure,' he said, 'but why is your face that peculiar colour?'

I had hoped that all traces of the salve had been eradicated after I had washed my face, but clearly that was not so. I explained what had happened.

'Let us hope that the dye is temporary,' Senguerdius declared. 'We can hardly compete in a disputation about witchcraft when one of our team looks like an oversized goblin.'

Fortunately Gerlach chose that moment to join us.

'I trust your face is soothed now, Master?' he asked.

'Thank you, much better. But I wonder if you can do anything about the green colour that people tell me has entered my skin?'

Gerlach seemed unconcerned. 'It will wear off anyway, but if it bothers you we can rub it with wine.'

'More wine?'

There was a jug of the stuff just a few feet away and I was sorely tempted to drench my head in it.

'Warm wine will be better,' Gerlach opined. 'The colour comes from plants that were steeped in wine, so if we add more wine the colour should go into the wine again, I'd have thought.'

This all seemed rather sketchy and optimistic to me, but since I am not a skilled apothecary and Gerlach was, I bowed to his opinion.

'Where did you learn your craft?' I asked him.

'I'm entirely self-taught,' he proclaimed, thus reducing my trust to its previous low level. In my book, self-teaching involves a lot of trial and error, and since there are many more wrong answers than right ones I was not confident of success, but I had no better ideas, so immediately after supper we returned to Gerlach's hut, where he warmed a ladle of wine over a lamp and swabbed my face with it.

I was gratified to see that the swabs were taking up some green colour, which suggested to my untutored mind that it must be coming off my face, and I am bound to admit that having one's face rubbed gently with warm wine is not unpleasant. Gerlach showed me my reflection in a small platter afterwards and not only was my skin healthily pink once more, but I looked quite a bit younger than the last time that I had seen my own face, with fewer wrinkles and smooth cheeks. Once when I was a young man in France I was shaved by a

Turk who used hot towels, and the effect was very similar. Naturally I have not repeated the shave, because it tended too much towards wanton luxury for my liking, but I could tell myself that the warm wine was medicinal, not the product of vanity. It was almost worth diving headfirst into a rose bush for.

One unlooked-for benefit of this diversion to the hut was that Senguerdius excused himself to write up some notes, so I was no wiser as to what the so-called "significant discoveries" might be, but that was a small price to pay for a few quiet moments and the chance to go to bed early where, sadly, sleep eluded me as I puzzled over Senguerdius' words.

In the morning I was up bright and early, though somewhat crestfallen to discover that the residents were all about already. I had thought I might have the place to myself for a while to think some more. I supposed that the library would be locked, but when I sauntered towards it I saw that the key had been obligingly left in the lock, presumably so that the first person to arrive could open it for the convenience of all, so I entered and began to peruse the shelves.

There were some treasures there. My examination of the day before had shown me some but a more leisurely look without Theodemar watching my every move demonstrated some magnificent volumes. There were texts in Greek and Hebrew, and even a couple in Arabic. I must get round to learning that language some day, I thought, wondering what I was missing as a result of my ignorance in the tongue.

Any scholars among my readers [*Van der Meer distinctly chuckled; he says he was clearing his throat, but I have my doubts*] will be able to imagine my delight when I found a copy of *De Docta Ignorantia* by Nicholas of Cusa on the shelves. I have long wanted to read this work, partly to see if Nicholas actually wrote some of the things commentators claim appear there. The title translates as *On Learned Ignorance* which refers to the idea that there is some knowledge that cannot be grasped by reason alone, however learned we are, and must instead be apprehended by intelligent speculation and revelation. In another work, Nicholas defended the need to advance knowledge by conjectures since reason alone will not reveal perfect knowledge of God and his ways. This notion appealed to me, since conjectures beyond reason were largely responsible for much of my success in solving crimes, but I had never read that book either, and since there did not appear to be a copy in the library I would have to go on guessing haphazardly.

I took the volume to a small desk and began reading it. It was absolutely fascinating, and I was so completely absorbed that I missed breakfast and was still reading when one of the Brothers came upon me.

'Master, they're waiting for you in the Hall!'

For a moment I had no idea who "they" might be, until it belatedly dawned on me that it must be ten o'clock and the debate was due to begin. I hurriedly pulled my gown about me, took up my cap and ran to the Hall to see if I could sneak into my seat. Of course, I could not; everyone was looking at the empty chair and von Anethan had a face like thunder as I rushed in. I mumbled an apology, then decided that since they were all scholars, honesty was the best policy.

'I am sorry, Your Grace, lady and gentlemen. I found a copy of a work by Nicholas of Cusa in the library and was engrossed. I apologise if I have kept you waiting.'

To my surprise, they all understood. I did not realise at the time, but the fact that Nicholas was a German and a Catholic was no bad thing, given that some German Catholics were in the room. Senguerdius even mumbled that it was a clever trick as I sat down, as if the mention of such a man were designed to influence the judges that even a Reformed scholar saw benefit in the works of Catholics.

Abbess Mathilde smiled. 'I must read it myself before I leave,' she said. 'Thank you for drawing our attention to it.'

Confound it, they only had one copy, and now I would not get to finish reading it.

Van Espen was a fine debater, one had to admit. He spoke easily and fluently, not confining himself to standing at the desk, but walking around, gesturing with his arms and repeating the key phrases of his argument to ensure that they were not missed. He possessed a pleasing voice and I had to remind myself that I could not just listen, but had to make notes rebutting his points. I might have thought that Senguerdius, being our lead speaker, would have been even more diligent in doing the same, but he sat with his arms folded, occasionally closing his eyes. I am not sure whether this was an aid to concentration or a method of gaining forty winks, but he showed no particular interest in recording any of Van Espen's speech beyond one point after about fifteen minutes when he found a place in his notes and wrote a small *punctus interrogativus* in the margin together with a word I could not read. To be perfectly honest, there was quite a lot of Senguerdius' notes that I could not read, because he scribbled quickly and with many contractions, though I am sure that if I had been left alone for a while in fair light I could have read them better. After all, I am very used to reading old handwritten documents. Believe me, good handwriting has never been a required gift for any philosopher or churchman, though I note that bishops are careful to write very legibly when money is concerned.

The timing of the debate was governed by von Anethan who had an hourglass before him. Thus he was to time eight hours, with breaks after every second hour. To prevent stealing of time, we were required to close our argument within two minutes of his tapping the floor with his crozier as the hourglass emptied a second time, and I found myself willing the sand to run faster. Willpower alone could not accelerate it, despite my best efforts, but I was hungry, having missed breakfast, and I needed to make water. For this purpose a screen had been erected at the back of the hall with, one presumed, a bucket behind it, but I will confess that I felt distinctly uncomfortable about using it in the presence of a lady, let alone a nun; and it was unthinkable that Abbess Mathilde should be subjected to such an indignity as having to sit on a bucket herself.

At length, von Anethan rapped on the floor twice, Van Espen concluded his paragraph and we all stood and bowed to the judges as they filed out to refresh themselves, and we followed. Mathilde was waiting by the door. I stood back to let her precede me, but she shook her head.

'Thank you,' she said, 'but when you've all gone I need to use the bucket.'

CHAPTER NINE

Very soon after we resumed, Van Espen sprang his surprise, inviting Friedrich Armand to come forward. Van Espen explained that because Armand did not speak Latin well, he proposed to question him in German, and would translate the questions and answers for us; unless, he said, bowing slightly, von Anethan wished to do so himself to ensure impartiality. Von Anethan waved the suggestion away haughtily, as if to say that just because he was a German it did not mean that he actually spoke German like a peasant would. His life was lived in Latin, and to emphasise the point he affected not to understand Armand's answers until Van Espen had translated them.

Van Espen began by asking Armand how he earned a living, at which Armand appeared to bristle and replied that his was not a living but a vocation. He was, he said, a witch-hunter.

'Indeed you are,' Van Espen agreed, 'and a most successful one! Tell us all about your experience.'

I had never met a real witch-hunter, and I am not sure that I have done so now, since Armand appeared to be full of bluster. He had, it seemed, been largely responsible for discovering most of the witches in the Rhineland, and quite a few further north too. He reeled off a list of towns and villages where witches had been found, extending even into Austria.

'He would have to go further afield,' Senguerdius whispered to me, 'now that many German authorities no longer believe in witchcraft!'

'Would it be fair to say that as a result of your activities,' asked Van Espen, 'a substantial number of witches have paid the penalty for their crimes?'

'I take no interest in the punishments,' Armand retorted. 'My role is only to detect and imprison these malefactors. It is for the proper authorities to determine their penalties as God gives them light to see their duty.' He blew his nose flamboyantly on a large red kerchief before continuing with a slight smile. 'It would be quite improper, I think, for a prosecutor to attempt to guide the judicial authorities in their responses.'

I wanted to stand up and shout at him that these were human beings who had been hanged, burned, branded or maimed because of his actions. And for what? For claiming to have supernatural powers that in reality they could only have if Almighty God granted them, in which event we would do well not to interfere in their activities.

If God is supreme then He can cancel any act of the Devil. If, then, the acts of witches displeased Him, He could prevent them or punish those who commit them, and I refused to believe that the likes of Friedrich Armand were the instruments of the Almighty in this respect.

Armand described in such a matter-of-fact way how he had taken some old women, stripped them naked, and had them examined by matrons for any signs of the Devil's teat through which imps or other evil offspring could be nourished. He laid great store on a book called *Malleus Maleficarum*, written two hundred years earlier by a Dominican named Kramer. If I tell you that the Bishop of Brixen expelled Kramer from his territories for insanity before he wrote this book, it says all I need to say about its reliability. I have never read it myself, because if I want to read lunatic ravings I can mark my undergraduates' essays.

The reader will forgive my indignation. These old women were no different to my grandmother. Now, I will grant that my grandmother had a sharp tongue and could be spiteful, but that is the way of old women. They speak before they think sometimes. If my grandmother — now, I hope, resting in heavenly splendour — had threatened someone with their milk curdling that would have been no more than a figure of speech. She had no powers to bring it about. Of course, I never saw her unclothed, but she probably had some warts somewhere that could be mistaken for the Devil's teat. Most old people have, I believe.

I was so annoyed that I forgot momentarily that we were there to win a debate, so it was fortunate that Senguerdius had heard this and was busily making notes.

'An hour or two in the library called for, Mercurius,' he muttered, by which I understood that he intended to attack Armand's evidence, or perhaps his credibility, when the time came. We had no right to cross-examine witnesses, but we could call them ourselves, and it may have been Senguerdius' intention to do just that.

Armand was now giving details of his first big witch hunt twenty years previously. When many parts of Christendom had abandoned witch hunts, he was just getting started, initially in the north, around the borders with the Danish kingdom. As he cleared one area of witches he moved on to the next, all the time obeying Kramer's injunction that since witches could not be reformed they must be burned as heretics. I think it is fair to say that I have never taken so quick a dislike to a man as I did to Armand. Nevertheless, his arguments had to be countered, and I hoped Senguerdius was going to do so, because I feared that my emotions might get the better of my logic if it were left until the fourth day when I would speak.

Given that Senguerdius had declared that our victory was certain before Armand began spouting his drivel I was surprised that my colleague was making such copious notes, and feared that he might be distracted from whatever clever argument he had already composed that, in his mind, made our victory certain.

'Give me your ink-horn, Mercurius. Mine's empty,' he commanded at one point, so I did as requested and held the empty horn up in the hope that someone would refill it. Brother Gilbert, who had charge of the library and scriptorium, duly obliged.

I have not mentioned Gilbert before; he was a small man, pale of complexion, no doubt as a result of spending too much time indoors. I should have placed him in his fifties, a man no longer needing his tonsure shaved because he had very little hair anyway. Gilbert had some Dutch, though he said he had not spoken it since childhood, it being the tongue of his father, but when his father died his mother had taken him to Burgundy where he grew up among her people.

I smiled and mouthed my thanks as Gilbert returned with the ink-horn, then realised that I had been day-dreaming and had missed some of Armand's testimony. Looking over Senguerdius' shoulder at his notes I could see that this must have centred on the probability that the daughter of a witch would herself be a witch; or, as Armand described it, the absolute certainty of it, for the demon's seed which produced a witch must necessarily be conveyed to all her children. Sons, possibly, he conceded, would be able to overcome this by rigorous self-mortification and religious devotions, but mere women, being weaker in all respects and known to be addicted to carnal delights, were certain to prove witches sooner or later, and therefore all female children of witches should be burned also, though he did not rule out humanely strangling them first, so long as the burning was conducted speedily before their malign spirit could infest some other person.

I have, in my long life, repeatedly heard this argument that women are addicted to pleasures of the flesh, which surprises me, because I have never yet met a single example who was. Even Fat Lysbeth owned that sometimes she did not feel like it, and endured intimacy rather than enjoying it. Now, it is possible that wanton women will not converse with someone like me who is known to be a minister of God, but surely at some stage in eighty years someone would have said something to me to support this assertion; and all common sense is against it, for congress leads to childbirth, and childbirth kills so many women. Who would entertain a hobby that has a good chance of leading to their death? I have heard it said that one in every forty women brought to childbed will die there; if that be so, then surely every woman must know another to whom this has happened, and therefore must surely fear the same for herself. And while her wifely duty must be to suffer her husband to lie with her, yet I cannot think that she would take any pleasure in it knowing that this may be the outcome.

Nevertheless, it is too widespread a belief for mere logic to overthrow it, and there seemed no prospect of convincing the judges otherwise for the only one who might understand the female mind, Abbess Mathilde, was a sworn virgin. I might, I suppose, have tried suggesting that if women are so addicted to intimate congress how could they willingly become nuns, but I must allow that this might only have caused the Abbess some embarrassment. Besides which, there are enough stories of depravity in convents to ensure that someone opposing me would quote one or two of them, if he were brave enough to risk Mathilde's displeasure.

This malign pattern of thought was happily interrupted by the rapping of von Anethan's staff on the floor to indicate that two hours had elapsed, so we rose and retired to the refectory where some food was ready for us. We were allowed an hour to refresh ourselves, though I could barely think of eating in view of my high emotion. I tried asking Senguerdius for his view of the morning's proceedings, but he motioned me to keep silent.

'We may be overheard, Mercurius. Let us keep our counsel until we have finished eating,' he said, then remained at table the entire hour, thus preventing my gleaning any information from him.

The cook, Brother Lodewijk, appeared in order to remove some of the emptied platters, which gave Senguerdius the opportunity to compliment him on his cooking. Senguerdius was hardly a gourmet, but those of us who had subsisted on Albrecht's fare for so long were inclined to be overly effusive when offered anything edible. Somehow Lodewijk had mastered the art of cooking even quite small birds so that they were cooked through without being incinerated, a skill that had bypassed Albrecht, and although I was not hungry I must confess that the small amount I ate was very palatable. Unfortunately Lodewijk's syllabub was merely very good, which meant it compared unfavourably with that of Albrecht's wife Mechtild. The alert reader may recall previous encomiums of mine on her sweets in general and her syllabub in particular, a fluffy yellow dish of heaven such as the angels must feast upon.

I suddenly felt very homesick.

By tacit agreement Armand had eaten in a corner with Theodemar and the almoner, Brother Simon, who by the nature of his work must be supposed to have more charity than most in his veins. Goodness knows he would need it to converse with Armand on any terms of civility.

When we resumed, Van Espen had only two more questions for Armand. The first concerned the reality of witchcraft. Were these women deluded, or did they genuinely commune with Satan? Needless to say, this was a pointless question, because Armand's opinion was no more valid than anyone else's, but Armand appeared to think hard before concluding that if there are good spirits, we cannot rule out the existence of evil ones, and therefore he was inclined to believe that there really were such evil entities with whom witches were in contact. I was tempted to interject that if Satan's agents were out and about, Germany is exactly the kind of place where you would expect them to be, but I restrained myself.

The second question was more subtle. Why, Van Espen asked, did women submit themselves to, and indeed worship, the evil powers rather than throwing themselves upon the mercy of Almighty God? The pedant in me noted first that he was assuming that the women were worshipping the Devil, which was the very thing that we were there to debate, so we must make sure to point that out to the judges at the first opportunity. As to the substance of his question, I could suggest an answer.

It is all very well for men to sit in monasteries and universities where they live, if not in luxury, at least in some comfort, and opine over the choices made by the wretched poor, who do not observe any great good in their lives and who seem to have missed out on God's bounty. I can imagine that if you have scratched a bare existence for sixty years, lost your husband, perhaps seen a child or two die, and have nothing to look forward to but pain, want and reliance on the charity of neighbours then the possibility of gaining some benefit in this life from an open-handed Satan might seem irresistible. I remember a minister telling me in shocked tones that he had reprimanded an old woman for prostituting her daughters and informed her sternly that she would go to Hell, at which she had replied that it was hard to imagine that Hell could be any worse than her current life. Of course, we ministers are experts on Hell, and we could tell her that it certainly will be worse, what with the little demons with red-hot pincers and sharpened stakes probing your fundament for all time, but these simple people lack the scholar's imagination, which is just as well, or they would live their entire lives beset with terror.

Armand had no doubt. Satan is real, and these women have had intercourse with him, and borne his imps, incubi and succubi, not to mention the occasional litter of kittens. Abbess Mathilde frowned at this last suggestion, while Dr Pfeiffer actually laughed, which seemed to irritate Armand.

'The learned doctor laughs,' he remarked, 'but I know what I have seen. It is not wise to doubt the power of the dark forces.'

'Oh, I do not,' replied Pfeiffer. 'But I may believe in the powers of Beelzebub and still doubt that humans can call upon them.'

'Let us not rush to judgement upon that point until we have heard all the evidence,' von Anethan suavely interrupted, and invited Armand to continue, but he seemed to have run out of things to say, and meekly resumed his seat.

I would have left him there. No, in truth at that moment I would have tied him to a millstone and rolled him into the

River Maas, were murder not a sin. Senguerdius, however, sprang to his feet.

'Learned judges,' he said, 'I beg to ask a question.'

'Please continue,' von Anethan directed.

'We may wish to call Herr Armand when we speak. Is it entirely proper for him to hear what is said here which may influence his opinions when questioned later?'

Von Anethan's face betrayed his surprise at the question, but then mine probably did too. He consulted with his fellow judges before issuing an opinion.

'We understand the question, but we think it would be discourteous to force Herr Armand to sit outside for three days just in case he is wanted. In any case, we think that a skilled debater like yourself would soon be able to detect any change of opinion on the gentleman's part and draw it to our attention, should such a thing happen.'

Senguerdius was hardly going to say that he was not clever enough to do so, and therefore he bowed and sat down.

'That's a pity,' I whispered.

'Not at all,' Senguerdius smiled. 'Did you notice von Anethan did not turn the hourglass on its side while the judges were conversing? Van Espen has lost above a quarter of an hour.'

When I preach — an admittedly rare event lately — I know that fifteen to eighteen pages will give me a sermon of forty to fifty minutes, so you can imagine how much material Van Espen had when I tell you that he came to the end of his eight hours with a few pages left. Uninterrupted, he might have continued another half an hour or so.

Von Anethan was about to close proceedings at the end of the first day when Senguerdius sprang to his feet again.

'By your leave, Your Grace, I have been reflecting on your remarks earlier, and it is clearly unfair to Herr Armand to keep him here longer than necessary. My colleague and I will confer soon, and if we have any need of Herr Armand I will address questions to him tomorrow, after which he will be free to return to his employment if Your Grace so directs. We would not wish to keep him from his paid work any longer.'

Von Anethan inclined his head in acknowledgement. 'Thank you, Professor Senguerdius. That is most accommodating of you.'

I caught a glimpse of Van Espen and Govarts out of the corner of my eye. Clearly they smelled some kind of rat, but were not quite sure what it was. It had not escaped my notice that under the rules of the debate any witness I introduced on the fourth day could not be brought back by the Leuven team, and I am sure that it had not escaped them either. Perhaps they suspected such a stratagem was in play here. If it was, I knew nothing about it, and I was just a little peeved that Senguerdius had said nothing to me before making his comment. It reinforced my view that we were a team only to the extent that Jesus Christ and the loaves and fishes were a team; that is, not at all.

At supper Armand again sat apart, attended only by Gerlach and another brother who turned out to be the treasurer, Ambrose. I had not been introduced to him, but had observed him lurking in the shadows since we arrived mentally computing the costs of having us there and hoping, no doubt, that any gifts we might collectively bestow on St Servatius would more than compensate.

I ate some fish and some black bread, a local speciality of the area which fortunately has not made its way to Leiden yet, and then tried some cheese before resolving to stick to raw fruit and vegetables for the rest of my stay in Maastricht. The beer was heavy and potent, and I could not drink much; which is to say that I should not have drunk much, but that fact only became apparent after I had drunk it. The effects were very strange, since my legs appeared not to function correctly and I unaccountably forgot the words of the Lord's Prayer at the evening service. On top of that, they must have given me a wobbly stool such that I fell off it at one point and bruised my knee, but I declined Gerlach's ministrations, having no wish to expose any other parts of my body to ridicule and green salve.

And so to bed.

CHAPTER TEN

I awoke to the definite feeling that those little demons I mentioned earlier were jabbing their miniature tridents into the backs of my eyeballs. Even sitting up was painful. On top of that I had a horrible taste in my mouth and my stomach was turbulent. I can only assume that the black bread didn't agree with me.

I rinsed my mouth and threw the window open to get some fresh air. It charged in as if it had been hanging around outside the shutters waiting for its chance. I felt quite light-headed with the sudden inrush.

The sounds of the kitchen at work told me it was time to get ready and go downstairs. When I tried to walk, I found that I seemed to have a limp, but then I discovered that I must have gone to sleep wearing one boot. I cannot account for this. [*Marginal note: Van der Meer says that he can. I shall not ask him, because whatever explanation his fevered mind has come up with, it is sure to be discreditable to me.*]

I do not like being seen before I have shaved, so despite my indisposition I set to with my razor and in a few minutes I was smoother of face, if you disregarded the multiple small cuts I gave myself. The rasp of the blade against my stubble seemed remarkably loud and made me jump at one point, but soon I was presentable and ventured downstairs, crossing to the chapel for the first prayers of the day.

Senguerdius was already there, kneeling piously surrounded by books with small strips of paper inserted between their pages. He must have been to the library, I thought, because he had not had so many volumes in his luggage.

Like many university lecturers Senguerdius believed that his favoured subject was fascinating to everyone else, so over breakfast he was musing aloud about the work of an Englishman called Newton, it being widely bruited abroad that Newton was on the verge of publishing a mighty work, as indeed he was. Little did we know, but it turned out that he submitted the first volume of his *Principia Mathematica* to the Royal Society that very week. Rumours had reached Senguerdius that Newton was expanding his ideas on celestial mechanics, whatever they are, and had concluded that an unseen force caused things to fall to the ground. The reader must understand that any deficiencies in this account are due to my splitting headache and my complete failure to comprehend what Senguerdius was talking about.

Anyway, it seems Senguerdius, whose first love was the natural sciences, had been considering the case of balloons. Our sailors travelling to the East Indies had returned with paper balloons, much prized by the Chinese, in which small candles were placed. When lit, these candles caused the balloons to fly upwards.

'Now, how do you explain that, then?' Senguerdius demanded of me.

'I have no idea,' I said. 'Enlighten me.'

'I have no idea either,' Senguerdius admitted, which was something of a letdown, as if a conjuror pulled away the cloth to reveal the dove still in the cage. 'But I mean to find out, Mercurius. As soon as I get back to Leiden, I intend to give it my full attention.'

This was rather concerning, because I thought he ought to have been giving his full attention to the affairs of the University, and I could not forebear reminding him that we had a debate to win.

'Pshaw!' he replied. 'It's in the bag.'

'Really?'

'Don't sound so surprised, Mercurius. I spent an hour in the library last evening and I am going to enjoy putting the fruits of my labours to that scoundrel Armand. Where is he, by the way?'

I looked around. Armand was not there, and now that my attention had been drawn to him I had to admit that I had not noticed him at prayers either.

'I'll wager he's slunk off to avoid the inevitable embarrassment he was about to endure at my hands, Mercurius.'

'I don't see how he can, Rector. The gates aren't open yet and there's a high wall round this compound.'

I sought out Theodemar and asked if he had seen Friedrich Armand. Theodemar made enquiries among the brothers and soon returned.

'He has not been seen. I must visit his chamber in case he is unwell.'

Senguerdius and I remained in the dining hall comparing notes and we were still there when Theodemar returned, looking concerned.

'He is not in his room, and his belongings are still there.'

'Has his bed been slept in?' I asked.

'That's right,' Senguerdius interjected. 'It's possible that he was one of those who were making so merry last night that they may have slept somewhere other than their chamber.'

I could not help but feel that this was somehow pointed at me, though I had been far from merry and had slept in my own bed.

'It had not,' Theodemar conceded.

'He's run off,' Senguerdius announced. 'Chicken!'

'I doubt he could climb the wall,' Theodemar commented, 'particularly in the dark. And we all saw him at supper, I think. I shall speak to the judges about a delay and organise a search party to scour the buildings and grounds for him.'

In the circumstances it was decided not to open the gates until he had been found. If any mishap had befallen him and a lady visitor happened upon his body it would be most unfortunate. It suddenly crossed my mind that we had a lady within the gates already, so I went in search of Abbess Mathilde to encourage her to remain in the hall.

'I am grateful for your concern, Dr Mercurius,' she replied, 'but I am not some silly little girl who has never seen death. Anyway, let us pray for his safe return to us rather than assume the worst.'

We both knelt to pray. It is surprising how intimate praying together can be in the right circumstances. Of course, the Abbess did not use perfumes or other worldly devices, yet there was such a sweet odour from her. As her hands were folded in prayer I noticed how pale her skin was, how smooth her hands, how long and elegant her fingers, with just a simple gold band on the ring finger of her right hand to show her spiritual marriage to Jesus. St Paul said that he did not permit a woman to have authority over a man, but I would willingly have submitted to Abbess Mathilde's authority. [No, Van der Meer, that is not a euphemism. I mean exactly what I said. Just write it down, and lower those eyebrows.]

We were interrupted by the arrival of Brother Gilbert, somewhat disturbed of countenance, who waited politely until we had finished our prayer and then asked if we knew where the Prior was.

'I haven't seen him since breakfast,' Abbess Mathilde replied. 'Is something wrong?'

'I wanted to borrow his key to the library,' Gilbert explained. 'I must have mislaid mine. I normally leave it in the lock out of hours and come back for it in the morning so that the brothers will not have to come looking for me when they want a book, but it isn't in the door now. Dear me, how careless I must have been!'

'Is the library locked?' I asked.

'Why, yes. That is why I need the Prior's spare key.'

'I believe the Prior is organising a search for Friedrich Armand,' I explained. 'He has not been seen this morning.'

To most of us, our first concern would have been for Armand's safety. It was clear from Brother Gilbert's face that his immediate assumption was that Armand had stolen some books and fled. Librarians are like that. Books are their friends, and people just a necessary inconvenience.

'Perhaps I ought not to disturb the Prior in that case,' Gilbert decided, 'since there are matters of such moment that he must attend to. I will wait.'

Given the size of the place and the many dark corners it contained, it must have been an hour or so before everyone returned to the dining hall to confirm that Armand could not be found.

'Has everywhere been searched?' demanded the Prior.

'I believe so,' Theodemar replied.

'Forgive me,' I interrupted, 'but Brother Gilbert was just telling us that the library is locked and he has not been able to enter.'

'Is this so?' asked the Prior.

'I'm afraid it is,' Gilbert said, his countenance turning even paler than it normally was. 'I must have mislaid the key after I locked it.'

'When did you lock it last?' I asked.

'Well, I suppose it would be yesterday morning. With so many people coming and going it seemed prudent. I hope it did not inconvenience anyone.'

'But it wasn't locked when I went in last night,' said Senguerdius.

'Ah, no,' agreed Gilbert. 'I unlocked it when the public left after the debate.'

'But you just told Dr Mercurius you last locked it yesterday morning?'

'Locked, indeed, yes; but I unlocked it later as I have just said. Forgive me, but the learned Doctor did not ask me when I last unlocked it.'

Senguerdius scratched his head in frustration. He clearly did not teach undergraduates as often as I did. 'So, if I understand you correctly, Brother Gilbert, you must have had the key last evening, and you would, according to your normal custom, have left it in the lock until morning.'

'Well, yes.'

'So the library should not be locked now?'

'That is what I came to say earlier,' he agreed.

The Prior produced his own keychain.

'Let us see for ourselves what has happened here.'

Many of us marched behind him to the library, where he attempted to put his key in the lock.

'That's odd. It won't go in fully and it won't turn,' the Prior announced.

Theodemar knelt and put his eye to the keyhole.

'There is a key in the other side,' he said.

'How can that be? Unless Armand took it himself and locked himself in...' said the Prior.

It was Theodemar who jumped to the obvious conclusion first. Hammering on the door he called out. 'Herr Armand! Herr Armand, are you in there?'

There came no reply.

'Should we break the door down?' Theodemar asked the Prior.

'I doubt we can,' the Prior replied. 'Look at the size of it. Let us send urgently for the locksmith.'

'Are there any windows?' Van Espen enquired, proving that he had not been to the library.

'None, I'm afraid,' Gilbert answered.

'And no other means of entry than this door?'

Gilbert gave this his full consideration for an appalling length of time before he replied. 'A very small child might conceivably climb down the chimney.'

'But that very small child would first have to ascend to the very top of the roof,' Theodemar pointed out. 'I think we can discount any such means of entry. No, the only way in is through the door.'

We waited in silence for the locksmith, the tension rising. I could see Abbess Mathilde and von Anethan retreat to the end of the corridor to say a rosary together.

The locksmith finally arrived and dropped to his knees to inspect the lock. 'Well, here's a pretty conundrum,' he murmured. 'How are we going to get you open then, Door?'

He jiggled the handle a bit. I could have told him that would not do the trick, since about a dozen of us had already tried it. Next he tried sliding a thin blade between the door and the doorpost to see if he could dislodge the metal tongue that sticks out into the frame. That did not work either.

'Could you saw that part off?' the Prior enquired.

'Look at the thickness of the metal,' said the locksmith. 'It'll take an age, even assuming I can find a blade thin enough to slide into that gap. No, we try something else.'

He delved into his bag for a long pair of tweezers which he carefully inserted in the keyhole.

'Maybe I can grip the wards of the key and turn it enough to unlock the door,' he explained. Suiting action to the word, he patiently threaded the ends of the tweezers into the hole and carefully lined them up. He applied increasing pressure and began slowly turning his wrist. There was a click and he withdrew his tweezers, now missing half of one leg. He said a word and then blushed as he realised that he probably ought not to have said it in front of a Bishop, an Abbess and a Prior.

'I'll get it yet,' he vowed, and introduced another device which, by some ingenious construction, became narrower at one end when you turned a screw at the other. Do not ask me to explain, or even to draw it. Using this he managed to grasp the key and turn it until eventually we heard the sound of the lock being withdrawn. In our eagerness to look in we almost trampled the poor fellow, but the Prior threw open the door, and we gasped.

Friedrich Armand was lying in the middle of the floor, face down but with his head turned slightly to the left, and the blood around it formed a ghastly halo that told us he was very much a dead man.

I dislike raising my voice, with the result that I spend much of my life being ignored. People poured into the room and charged towards Armand's corpse without any thought for what they were doing, so that I was obliged to shout at the top of my voice.

'Stand still!'

Let us give credit to them all because they did exactly as I asked.

'Forgive me, but I have some experience of the investigation of crimes. We must be careful not to obliterate any footmarks or other evidence that will reveal who the assailant might be.'

'Assailant?' asked Gilbert. 'Someone has done this to him?'

'Well, he's hardly done it himself, has he?' Senguerdius remarked. 'For a start, I see no weapon that might account for that wound. When a man harms himself the instrument of his destruction must surely be at hand when he is discovered.'

There was much mumbling and crossing of oneself going on.

'No doubt the mayors must be informed,' von Anethan said, 'but, in the meantime, I think we would do well to lean on Dr Mercurius for guidance.'

The Prior seemed uneasy. 'Since this is church property, Your Grace, and it seems likely that the perpetrator is here among us, I should prefer Dr Mercurius to make such an inquiry. Relationships with the civic authorities are not always harmonious and if we open the gates to allow outsiders to enter we risk the escape of the man responsible.'

This mix of disdain for the civil authorities, sturdy self-reliance of the church and a modicum of common sense must have impressed von Anethan, because not long after the Prior was invited to become a bishop somewhere. To my way of thinking, bishops are a bit like privies; we have to have some, though we don't like to talk about them, and you don't want to have too many close together, when they can be a real nuisance.

Von Anethan was looking at me with the sort of look that bishops reserve for would-be seminarians when assessing them for ministry.

'Mercurius, will you take on this task?' he asked.

'If you so wish, Your Grace,' I said, as humbly as I could given my belief that nobody else in the room had the least idea where to start an inquiry. Then, feeling that tact might smooth my path, I added, 'And since Father Prior is agreeable.'

I said a quick prayer before acting. I do not know whether it helps, but when a churchman bows his head in prayer people stop asking him questions or making stupid suggestions.

'May I ask you all to take a couple of paces backwards to clear a space around Armand? Please look carefully for anything on the floor as you do so.'

To my amazement they all did as I had asked. Nothing of any importance was found; that is, Brother Simon found a button under a stool, but it did not match Armand's clothing.

'Perhaps he ripped it off the clothing of his assailant,' Simon suggested.

I was doubtful. 'I see no signs of a struggle, Brother Simon.'

'Yet the expression on Armand's face bespeaks great fear,' Govarts observed.

I had not yet walked to the other side of the body but having done so I could see what Govarts meant. On the other hand, expressions are hard to read. Perhaps he was merely in great pain?

'We have here a man whose head has been damaged by some heavy object with a sharp edge,' I remarked, for one side of the wound was straight as if sliced with a blade. 'Whatever did it must be marked with blood or brain. Let us look around the library for any object so marked.'

'It might be under his body,' Van Espen suggested.

'It might,' I conceded, 'but before he is moved we need to make a sketch of the body as it lies so that we do not have to resort to fallible memories. Is there anyone here skilled in drawing?'

I looked at the Prior, but he looked quite helpless, as if none of the brothers had the least idea how to draw.

'I would be willing to try.'

The voice was unexpected, and the crowd parted to disclose its source. Abbess Mathilde was walking forward. Like many well brought-up women, art was part of her education, I suppose.

'It is hardly fitting...' von Anethan began, but she silenced him by simply raising her hand.

'I am not unaccustomed to death, Your Grace. And this is a service that I can render to our poor deceased brother, and therefore I should. Is it not the Christian thing to do?'

Put like that, we could hardly argue.

CHAPTER ELEVEN

On the motion of the Prior, all withdrew from the library to pray for the soul of the lately departed Armand, except myself, Abbess Mathilde, and von Anethan who insisted on remaining in case she succumbed to feminine frailty and fainted. I saw no sign that she was in danger of doing so. Instead, she sat upon a stool slightly behind his feet on his left side so that her drawing would include his face. Having completed that with commendable rapidity and accuracy, she then suggested that she should draw the wound so that we would have a permanent reminder of its appearance.

'Is that really necessary?' von Anethan demanded.

'If we do not, then we can hardly bury him until we have found the weapon,' she explained, thus doing my job for me. I had started to think along those lines but had not quite formulated the thought into a sentence. I had, however, formulated another sentence for von Anethan, but if I had voiced it aloud I would have been excommunicated for saying such a thing to a bishop. Fair comment on a matter of public interest is not a defence likely to prove successful in the Catholic Church where abuse of a bishop is concerned.

We carefully lifted Armand and turned him over, the better to see the wound. It was exceedingly ugly. It began slightly in front of his right ear and extended around a hand's span upward towards the crown of the skull. There was a lot of blood which would have to be washed off carefully in due course, but the front edge of the wound was very straight, the rear edge less so. The front had penetrated about the thickness of two thumbs, pushing the skull before it. Whatever implement had done this must have been swung with great force by a very strong man — or, conceivably, a demon.

I left Abbess Mathilde drawing while I examined the button that Brother Simon had found. It was a very ordinary button made of horn and painted black. This might sound quite distinctive, but I could immediately think of half a dozen of us who were wearing garments that might have had such a button, including myself; and there was always the possibility that it had nothing to do with the crime and had been there for days beforehand.

I will confess that I had not liked Armand. He was boastful and arrogant, but if we allow people to go around killing anyone boastful and arrogant the streets would be much less crowded and the next papal conclave would be very short of electors. Besides which, nobody deserves to die in such a way. It must have been mercifully quick, I suppose, but surely painful and terrifying. How awful it must be to realise that you are about to die; no wonder his face looked so anguished.

Lacking windows as it did, the library was naturally gloomy, but nobody could have sneaked out as we entered. I came out to ask for more lights to be brought so that we could examine the scene more closely, and met Senguerdius coming towards me.

'Have prayers finished?' I asked.

'I didn't go. It was all a bit Roman for my liking, so I said some myself in private, then thought perhaps I could be of some assistance. Two heads are better than one, after all.'

Not just two heads, I thought; his was one of the finest brains in Europe. I could only profit by hearing the fruits of his ruminations.

'It's baffling,' I admitted. 'A man dies by violence when he is alone in a locked room with the key on the inside of the lock.'

'Then he cannot have been alone,' said Senguerdius.

'But no-one left,' I protested.

'No human being,' Senguerdius replied, 'but who is to say that there was not an invisible demon or spirit there?'

'Have you ever seen an invisible spirit?' I asked.

'Of course not. They're invisible. You can't see them.'

'I mean, have you ever heard a convincing narrative that suggests that such a thing might exist?'

'No,' admitted Senguerdius, 'but if we allow the existence of the Holy Ghost it is logically inconsistent not to accept the possibility of an Unholy Ghost too.'

He had something there, I had to admit.

'But this is consecrated ground. Have you heard of a malevolent spirit daring to venture into such a space?'

Senguerdius considered this for a moment. 'The church is consecrated, certainly; and the church precincts may be. But perhaps the library is a later addition. Or maybe if it isn't used for holy purposes the consecration wears off. Alternatively, perhaps some of our Protestant brethren are right when they say that the whole world is the Lord's and no one part is any holier than any other.'

I felt a shiver running down my spine. I had been taking comfort in the thought that holy spaces were safe from the Devil's agents, and I did not like to think that I could find myself face to face with the forces of darkness. I once met a French Cardinal and that was creepy enough for me.

I decided to try a different tack. 'But what reason could there be for killing him?'

Senguerdius shrugged. 'He's a witch-finder. Presumably Satan doesn't want his witches found. And don't forget that he was about to leave to resume his searches. While he was here he wasn't actively opposing the Devil, but as soon as he said he was going home, the Devil needed to act to stop him.'

'How would the Devil know all that?'

'The Devil knows everything, I suppose, except the mind of God. It is hard to imagine that he cannot read our thoughts. After all, doesn't Satan use our hidden weaknesses to attack us? He knows what will work for each of us.'

'So you think Armand was killed by some kind of demon or sprite sent by Satan?'

'I believe in the use of our reason, Mercurius. Can you think of a better way to explain how a man can be murdered in a locked room by a killer who can escape leaving the door locked behind him on the inside?'

Extra lanterns having been brought, I returned to the library and began a careful search of the room. The Prior had assured me that there were no hidden doors or secret passageways, which meant, of course, that there were no such passageways that he knew of. I asked Senguerdius to look for any books or mouldings that might operate secret levers. Govarts and Van Espen had also offered their services so I set them to measuring the buildings carefully so we could determine where there might be spaces in the walls that could hide an assassin if such a concealed door existed. Meanwhile I walked round the perimeter looking for signs that a shelf had moved forward or pivoted. Any concealed room must be dusty, I thought, so a collection of dust might be suspicious.

I found no such dust, nor scratches on the floor suggesting shelves had been moved. What I did find were droplets of blood. There were several by the door, and none in the corners to either side. That suggested that the wounded Armand had tried to escape but had failed to do so and had retreated to the middle of the room to die. Or perhaps the Demon had gathered up some blood and sprinkled it in some kind of diabolical ritual?

I stopped to think hard. A beer at Steen's Inn would have been very welcome now, partly because it would have helped me to think, but mainly because it would place me about 140 miles from here. If Satan had done this I didn't want to prove it and upset him, in which case 140 miles would be nowhere near enough distance to escape him.

Just a minute, Mercurius, I said to myself. *You came here to disprove superstition. Your whole argument was that witches cannot possess the powers that others claim they have. Why allow them those powers now?*

That's a very good question, I told myself. *I must proceed as if the Devil is not the killer, and look for some earthly murderer. Only if I cannot prove a case against one can I allow myself to place the blame on the Devil.*

Govarts and Van Espen had done their calculations and came to report that they could find no possible spaces in the walls where anyone of normal size might hide. Careful measurement had convinced them that the walls were precisely as thick as you would expect a wall to be. At most, something the size of a small cat might have squeezed between the layers of brick at the end opposite the door of the library. I thanked them for their conclusions, which I had no reason to question, and squatted in the library looking into Armand's blank staring face. I had not seen such a look of bewildered incomprehension since I tried to explain the history of the doctrine of the Trinity to my class.

Needless to say, the conversation that I had conducted with Senguerdius was preying on my mind, with the result that I found myself reflecting on the example that Govarts and Van Espen had used. The Devil is alleged to be able to disguise himself as a cat, usually a black one. Could he have metamorphosed into such an animal and hidden behind the library wall? But then, how had he passed through the solid wall into the library when we could find no opening? [Van der Meer suggests that the Devil could just walk through a wall, which I suppose might be true, but then he would not need to convert into feline form first. Not that we knew for sure that he did, of course. Why can't Van der Meer just wait until the end of my account and then all will be revealed? Or not, because if he keeps interrupting I may forget something.]

I took up Abbess Mathilde's sketches and compared them to the sight before me. They were quite good for an amateur, though obviously not of the quality that Vermeer would have given me, if he had not inconveniently died a decade or so earlier. You could almost see the texture of the hair…

Just a moment!

Where was his cap? The brothers often went bare-headed but everyone else wore some kind of cap or hat. Even Senguerdius, who often did not bother at the University, had adopted a square academic cap to go with his robes. Armand himself wore a soft black cap made of some kind of fur with a small peak at the top of the head. I searched the library assiduously for that cap but could not find it anywhere. Why would the assailant make off with his hat? And, to add to the mystery, how had he spirited it through a locked door? I suppose it was just possible that Armand had taken it off when we were not around, but just in case I asked the Prior to invite everyone to keep an eye out for that cap.

The brothers arrived with a large canvas sheet to take Armand to Gerlach for washing and preparation for his funeral. The Prior supervised to ensure that all was done with due reverence, and began by saying a few sentences from a funeral vigil. The brothers chanted Psalm 129 (by the Catholic reckoning), *De profundis clamavi ad te, Domine*; Out of the depths have I called to you, O Lord. Considering that the Christian gospel is one of joy, it never ceases to surprise me that we are so good at creating a sense of misery in our worship, though I suppose if you are going to be glum, a funeral is a good time to do it.

After the Magnificat was sung the Prior asked for absolution of Armand's unconfessed sins, and all fell silent until he gestured for the brothers to step forward. Lying the canvas beside Armand, each took a limb. Ordinarily someone would have supported the head, but I could understand why nobody was keen to touch that gory mess. At the Prior's command they lifted the corpse and carefully laid it on the canvas. My attention was so fixed on that sight that I did not react at first when the Prior spoke.

'There is his cap, Dr Mercurius,' he said, pointing to the floor. It must have been under his body and had not been revealed when we turned him on his back.

The brothers bore Armand away, and the Prior asked if he might send someone to clean the floor before it was permanently stained.

'I see no reason why not,' I answered. 'Thank you for your ready assistance today. I am sorry that this has been visited upon you and your house.'

'*Sobrii estote, et vigilate: quia adversarius vester diabolus tamquam leo rugiens circuit, quaerens quem devoret*,' he replied.

It took me a moment to realise that he was quoting from the Bible, to be precise, from the first letter of St Peter, chapter 5, verse 8; *Be sober, be vigilant; because your adversary the Devil, as a roaring lion, walketh about, seeking whom he may devour.*

All this talk of the Devil was quite unnerving. I am quite sure that the Devil is responsible for fewer violent deaths than naughty men with big sticks. If Armand had been found in the street nobody would even have suggested that Satan was behind his killing. It was just the unusual circumstance of his body being found in a locked room that made people think of the Evil One.

Though, I had to admit, finding any alternative explanation was proving to be beyond me just at that moment.

I picked up the cap and turned it around in my hands. There was a large patch of blood on the right side, presumably corresponding with the wound that we had seen. There was another soggy mess at the top of the cap that might, perhaps, have been caused by the cap lying in a pool of blood. If I looked closely I might have been able to persuade myself that there was more blood on the outside than the inside there, whereas the opposite was true of the mark over the wound.

Presumably the cap fell off when Armand hit the ground. I could imagine him writhing in pain for a short while before he died, although he might equally well have been killed at the moment the blow was struck. Who could tell? Yet I remember being told by Dr Drelincourt when he was Rector that the dead do not bleed, so to shed so much blood he must have lived for a while after the blow. He may, of course, have been insensible as his life ebbed away. One could only hope, for his sake, that such had been the case.

Von Anethan would have called for a day of fasting in memory of Armand had it not been for the fact that the kitchens had already prepared the dinner, and to waste it seemed luxurious, so we settled down to eat without any great enthusiasm, at least not on my part. I nibbled some bread and took a bowl of bean soup, but my appetite had flowed away as surely as Armand's blood.

It was not helped by Senguerdius' conversation. I have heard it said that people who have an optimistic outlook on life tend to live longer, in which event it is no surprise that Senguerdius is still alive as I write this and, if the saying is true, he can expect to live another hundred years or more, for I never knew a man less likely to be deflected by the buffeting life gives us from time to time.

In contrast to my picking at my food, Senguerdius was making short work of a large piece of duck when he ruined what little appetite I had.

'I'm not unaware, Mercurius, that you have brought much honour to the University in the past by your service of the Stadhouder and your remarkable record in solving mysteries.'

'Thank you,' I said politely, though I was highly suspicious about where this was leading.

'And I have no doubt that given your splendid ability in such matters, you will bring this affair to a successful conclusion, despite the obvious handicap.'

'Handicap? What handicap?'

Senguerdius eyed me up and down as if he thought I might be jesting with him. 'Why, the fact that the gates were bolted and therefore the killer, if a human being, must be sitting round this table now,' he murmured.

'Ah, yes, I'd realised that,' I said.

'But despite this you have allowed everyone here to help in some way. I must admit, I would have gone wrong on that point because I would not have accepted help from anyone until they had been cleared of suspicion in case they tampered with the evidence, but you have cunningly lulled the murderer into a false sense of security. Very clever of you, Mercurius.'

I tried to speak with a crust of bread hanging out of my mouth, which must have looked inelegant and caused me to undergo a fit of coughing. 'Would you mind expanding on that?' I croaked.

'Well, take Abbess Mathilde, for example. If she were the murderer she could have omitted something important from the drawings she did for you.'

'But she's a nun,' I stammered.

'Well spotted. I wondered why she was wearing that funny outfit. And your point is…?'

'Well, she's a nun.'

'I think we've established that point, Mercurius.'

'A woman.'

'Ah, I see what you mean. I should have said "If she were the murderess…", shouldn't I?'

'No. Well, yes. But what I meant was — if we can't trust nuns, whom can we trust?' I said plaintively.

'What an interesting way of looking at things,' Senguerdius said. 'You are hypothesising that a nun is, by virtue of her calling, prohibited from being a murderess?'

'No. Well, yes. Sort of. Up to a point.'

'Mercurius, a definitive statement cannot be "up to a point". Either she cannot be a murderess or she might be. Do you have any evidence one way or the other?'

'Just look at her,' I answered. 'She doesn't look like a murderess.'

Senguerdius did as I had bidden. Slightly awkwardly, Mathilde caught him looking and smiled at him.

'I don't have your experience in this field,' he announced. 'What do murderers look like?'

I thought of those I had known. Actually, there weren't that many.

'They've all been men,' I replied.

'But women do commit murders?'

'Undoubtedly. One need only think of Countess Báthory seventy years ago.'

Elizabeth Báthory and some of her servants were accused of murdering up to 650 girls at her estate in Hungary. According to the more lurid accounts she killed young virgins so she could repeatedly bathe in their blood and thus preserve her beauty. There are obviously more virgins in the average Hungarian village than in the comparable Dutch ones. Where I grew up I think you would have struggled to collect enough virgins' blood to fill a bath once. However, I digress.

'If women commit murders, then logically,' Senguerdius pressed home, 'we have no reason to suppose that Abbess Mathilde cannot commit murder.'

'But she's a nun,' I bleated.

'You seem somewhat fixated on this point, Mercurius. We have established her vocation and I am happy to concede that she is, in fact, a nun.'

I must confess that I could not imagine those elegant and slender fingers wielding any implement that could cause death.

'Surely she hasn't the strength to cause Armand's wounds?' I answered. It sounded quite a feeble protestation even as I uttered it.

'Mercurius, do you have any sisters?'

'No, Rector.'

'Other close female relatives?'

'My mother, obviously. And one of my grandmothers lived with us.'

'And you still maintain that women lack the necessary strength? Did you ever see your mother or grandmother in a passion?'

He had me there. In my mind I could clearly see my grandmother giving my grandfather a piece of her mind when I was very small after he sold an animal at the market and then spent much of the proceeds at the inn before returning home. I had been so scared of her I had hidden in the cowshed until supper, and I hadn't been the one who had squandered the money. If Grandfather hadn't been so drunk that he didn't understand what she was saying he would surely have been frightened too. As it was he lay down by the stove to sleep it off and continued to do so despite several kicks in the ribs from a dainty foot, albeit one wearing a clog. That particular grandfather died not many years after. I do not think she killed him; he probably decided his life would be easier if he just died quietly.

'I take your point,' I said.

'And if she can be the murderer, then so can anyone here, except you, I suppose.'

When he put it like that, I thought that I could not even be sure of my own innocence.

I dropped the bread on my platter and took a deep draught of beer. Maybe Grandfather's way of dealing with life's problems had something to commend it after all.

CHAPTER TWELVE

When dinner ended I raced to find Brother Gerlach. I admit that my idea was to burst in on him without any notice just in case he was manipulating the corpse. In the event, he was carefully washing Armand's body, which was now naked, a small square of white linen precisely placed to protect his modesty.

As he worked he recited the prayers for the dead, stopping for a moment when he first saw me, but then continuing until he had finished before speaking to me.

'Your face has healed well, Master.'

'Thanks to you.'

'God does the healing. I just use whatever poor gift He has given me.'

I walked to the top of the table and inspected the head.

'That's a really nasty wound,' I said.

'Worse than you think,' agreed Gerlach. 'Try pressing on the head just above the ear.'

I did so, and recoiled in horror. 'It goes right in!'

'I suspect if I were permitted to open it I would find that a portion of skull has become completely detached.'

'Does that mean two blows, one in front and one behind?'

'Not necessarily. It might speak of a weapon wide enough to cause that scalp wound with one blow. I see no signs that the head has been struck twice, now that I have washed the blood away.'

However, with the body stripped another wound was visible.

'What has happened to his arm?'

'I think it has been injured by trying to fend off a blow.'

'It's his left arm.'

'So it is, Master.'

I turned back and forth as I tried to visualize the sequence of events. 'So he was hit on the arm, then turned and was struck from behind?'

'That is possible,' Gerlach admitted, 'but who would turn his back on an assailant? Surely it is more likely that the first blow was struck from behind, then Armand turned to face his attacker and used his arm to defend himself against a second blow.'

'And there was no third blow?'

Gerlach shrugged. 'It seems not.'

'So he just lay down to die?'

'That blow to the head must have stunned him, Master. He might have retained enough awareness to raise his arm but it may have been automatic, in the same way that an animal raises a paw when attacked.'

'Stunned him? But it didn't kill him outright?'

'He would not have bled so long if he had died immediately.'

That tallied with my own idea.

'There were some drops of blood near the door. Could he have been struck there and crawled to the place where he was found?'

Gerlach shook his head. 'It's hard to picture such a thing. Surely the drops were just spray from the blow, either pumped from the wound or shaken off the weapon on the second strike.'

I could see how that might be, but now another question occurred to me. 'So if blood sprayed like this, it is likely that the attacker was spattered as well?' I asked.

Gerlach paused to rinse his cloth. 'A man would, I think. But as for a demon, who knows whether any laws of nature apply to them? Surely one who can walk through locked doors can escape an asperging with his victim's blood?'

The intelligent reader, if I have any, will immediately spot the difficulty with this line of argument. If every piece of evidence was going to be questioned along the lines of "A human being would do such-and-such, but different rules apply to demons" we were not going to get very far.

However, I had to concede that any human agency in this murder was rather hard to uphold given the absence of a weapon behind the locked door. I know that the powers of darkness are alleged to be able to do many things, including a few apparently impossible ones, and I would not have been surprised if a vote of those I had left in the hall had shown a widespread belief that walking through locked doors was child's play for a disembodied malevolent spirit, but I had never heard that they could take a material object such as a weapon with them. The implement that had inflicted these wounds must still be in the library, whether the killer was a human being or a ghostly presence. Maybe we had not recognised it as a weapon? Was there anything that might have been cleaned and returned to its previous place?

'Could you inflict this injury with a book?' I asked.

'A book?' Gerlach asked in reply.

'Yes. You know, a big thing with words in it.'

'I can't think of any book that we might have that could do this, at least not without suffering serious damage itself.'

'There are one or two locked books with metal clasps,' I suggested.

'There are,' conceded Gerlach, 'but I should have thought it very difficult to wield a book so that the clasp comes down on someone's head. And even if you could, the leather it is attached to is softer than the skull, so surely the book would be visibly damaged.'

'Perhaps it is,' I mused. 'I'd better go back to the library and look again. What about one of the fireplace tools?'

'Not a poker — that would be too narrow to inflict a wound two thumb-widths wide.'

'Even if he struck two or three times?'

'Think of the precision that would be required, Master. When I chop wood, I take my time but I still have difficulty putting my axe exactly where I want it.'

'Ah — an axe?'

Gerlach rubbed his chin. 'I suppose it might be possible, but it would need to have a thick blade compared with the length of its face. And someone walking through these buildings with an axe would provoke comment, surely? We certainly don't keep one in the precincts.'

'It's quite a puzzle,' I admitted.

'So it is, Master. But we all have faith that if anyone can solve it, you can,' Gerlach announced.

They may have had faith. I didn't.

Senguerdius was in the library when I got there, sitting reading at a desk.

'Ah, there you are, Mercurius! Solved the problem yet?'

'Not yet,' I confessed. 'What are you reading, Rector?'

'Hm? Oh, a remarkably ill-informed book about the elephant.'

I might have hoped that he had been bending his considerable brain around the question of who killed Armand, but it seemed that I was on my own there.

'I've never seen an elephant, Mercurius, so I am not able to verify or contradict this account. But this writer makes claims about the size of such an animal that seem unlikely. Natural science defies his description.'

Senguerdius launched into a lengthy monologue about the strength of animal thighbones, the size of their feet and how the sun strikes our skin and warms our blood. So much I captured, but it was interwoven with learned argument and a display of mathematics — never my strongest subject — that left me unsure what had just been proved incontrovertibly to me or, indeed, what the question was that Senguerdius had been answering in the first place.

Speaking of whom, Senguerdius was obviously waiting for some kind of response from me.

'I bow to your knowledge, Rector,' I said, one of those all-purpose sayings that means everything and nothing and has got me out of many a tedious discussion with Rectors over the years. All too often I found myself pondering on the etymology of the words "Rector" and "rectum" and wondering if there was a connection. Curiously, the man who could definitely have answered that question was one of those in whose presence the question came to mind most frequently.

I began looking for books or other objects large enough and sufficiently heavy to have been the weapon that killed poor Armand. Whatever it was would surely be bloodstained, but none of the books seemed to be, and many were simply too small to be implicated. I became excited for a while when I found blood on the corner of a stool and wondered whether this might be the weapon, but when I showed it to Senguerdius he was unimpressed.

'Isn't that the mark of a hand?' he asked.

Now that I looked at it again, I could see his point. Armand must have tried to raise himself up by pushing on the stool.

'I've been thinking, Mercurius,' Senguerdius began. I say began because that was all he said before clamming up again.

'Yes, Rector?'

'No, you don't need the ravings of an amateur given your considerable experience of these matters.'

'I'd be interested to hear what you have to say,' I insisted. It was true, too. Any glint of light would have been welcome at this point.

'Why do you think he was killed at night?' Senguerdius enquired.

I thought hard. 'There was nobody around to interfere with the murderer's plan, I suppose,' I said.

'But on the other hand a cry for help would surely be more readily heard in the silence.'

'True, but there wasn't a cry for help.'

Senguerdius smiled and raised an admonitory finger. 'We don't know that. We know that no-one claims to have heard it, which is a different matter. Of course, the murderer would have heard it, but he would lie to save his neck. Or her neck.'

'Surely no woman could have done this!' I gasped.

'Let's keep an open mind,' Senguerdius replied. 'But the point I'm making is that the murderer could not have known that nobody would hear a scream.'

'I will grant that.'

'And he would have found it harder to see his victim. Did you observe any candle in the library when we broke in?'

'No, but surely it could have burned away during the night.'

'It could, but it had to be in some kind of holder, and I saw none. I remember because when we were searching the floor I looked for a candle to help me see into the corners. With no light the library must have been very dark.'

'Indeed.'

'So, given the difficulties that the killer gave himself, I draw the conclusion that he attacked in the evening because it was the only time that he could attack.'

'Meaning?'

'Perhaps the killer is one of those entities that only walks by night.'

There are times in the life of a lecturer when I think that the University of Leiden is far too enlightened for its own good, since it forbids teaching staff to horsewhip stupid students. I have therefore perfected a scornful look which, on this occasion, I was too shocked to deploy.

'I thought you didn't believe in witches and demons,' I protested.

'I don't,' Senguerdius allowed. 'But I may be wrong.'

I was ambling back to the library deep in thought when Theodemar accosted me as I passed the treasury.

'Ah, Dr Mercurius! The Bishop was hoping to have converse with you before Vespers.'

When bishops call, the wise man responds promptly, even if they are not your own bishop. They can make your life miserable if you upset them, which was why the ensuing discussion was so unpalatable.

'Thank you for waiting upon me,' von Anethan said surprisingly graciously, considering he was one of the German bishops, who are not renowned for their sensitivity.

'I came as soon as I could,' I replied.

'Of course,' said von Anethan, as if it were unthinkable that anyone would keep a bishop waiting. 'Dr Mercurius, I just wanted to clarify something. I came here expecting to be away from my diocesan duties — which are quite onerous — for about a week. When do you think I might be able to leave?'

If you're the murderer, I thought, *the authorities normally allow three days between sentence and execution, to give you some time for repentance.*

'I recognise, naturally, that you will require us to remain here until you have solved this horrible crime,' he added, 'so I suppose I am asking when you expect to have done so.'

'There are … particular difficulties about the circumstances that make this case especially testing,' I replied, without specifying what those were, since I had not yet dreamed any up. 'I continue to pray for God's guidance.'

'As do we all,' said von Anethan fervently, and I had no reason to doubt his enthusiasm to see the right person hanged for this, if only because it meant that he would not be the one on the end of the rope. Somewhat oddly, I found myself wondering how one hangs a demon, and whether it was likely to kill him or not. After all, if you are permanently undead, hanging you presents some problems. Not to mention that a noose that encircles a man's neck would prove inadequate if he then transmuted himself into, say, a cat.

'Let us hope that you are able to bring this sorry matter to a close promptly,' von Anethan said. 'I look forward to celebrating Mass on Sunday and leaving shortly afterwards. You will know where to find me if you need me thereafter.'

He walked away before I could answer. Today was Wednesday. That broadly left me three days to pull off a miracle. I know Jesus Christ did some sharp work in three days, but I am not He. [Van der Meer just sucked air through his teeth. Asked to explain himself, he said that he was not sure that I should commit blasphemy in these pages. What is blasphemous about anything that I have said? Every time we say the Creed we testify that Jesus Christ rose again on the third day, so it's a bit rich to complain about my saying so here. And I distinctly said I am not Christ, which is an indisputable fact. Van der Meer says he is worried that any comparison may be inappropriate. Well, I would compare Van der Meer to a horse's backside, but the comparison may be offensive to horses.]

I attended Vespers, but I was not in the right frame of mind. I was looking around the chapel for any object that might make a suitable weapon, and resolved to grab a quick peek at the heavy golden candlesticks on the altar before they were returned to the treasury. There was no sign of blood or damage on them. In any event, they would surely have been locked away when the murderous assault took place.

The Psalm had announced that *I lift up my eyes to the hills; the hills from whence comes my help*, which was not very encouraging in so flat a country. As it happened, we were about a day's walk from the highest point in the land at Vaalserberg, but it is not really a mountain and I could not see it from Maastricht anyway. Still, it was worth a try, so I went outside, worked out my bearings and knelt down, saying a prayer before raising my head. A passing pigeon spattered me. That seemed a fitting summary of my day.

I wish I could say that in the couple of hours between Vespers and Compline I made a major breakthrough in this matter, but the truth is that I retired to my room to clean myself up and then sat on my bed and whimpered.

If the forces of darkness were abroad in this place perhaps I should get some sleep in daylight, I thought, because I will not dare to do so at night. I was also concerned that Senguerdius, no doubt with the best of intentions, had been telling everyone about my previous triumphs and assuring them that my efforts would be crowned with success, observing that he might hang on a few days after a satisfactory resolution to watch the miscreant pay for his sins on the gallows. This was not because Senguerdius was a bloodthirsty fellow. It was more that he felt that detection was only a necessary preliminary before the climax of the episode, the expiration of the sin. Added to which, he had a theory about the mechanism of hanging that he wanted to test out, for which purpose he needed a criminal who would consent to be weighed and measured in the interests of natural philosophy. Senguerdius was inclined to suppose that if you made the criminal wear heavy chains about his person when he was hanged you need not build a gallows so tall, which would be a great saving in time and materials. It would be more humane too, because the victim would die quicker, as when men hasten the end of a malefactor by hanging on his legs.

No matter how many times I turned the matter over in my head, puzzles remained. Apart from the obvious one about a door locked from the inside, I also wanted to understand what had happened with Armand's cap. It cannot have been dislodged in the attack, because it was saturated with blood at the place where the wound was, so why does a dying man remove his cap and lie on top of it? Or had the perpetrator done it for him, and if so, why?

Armand had been killed sometime between the end of supper and bedtime the night before, but that was quite a small period of time. Whether he had attended Compline or not the whole place goes to bed once it is finished and the chapel has been tidied. The entire thing might take forty minutes, and we knew that Armand had not gone to bed with the rest of us because he had not slept there. He could, conceivably, have hidden somewhere and prowled around in the night hours, but, as Senguerdius had noted, he did not have a candle or lantern, and in this tangle of rooms and corridors it was hard to see how someone who was not a resident of the complex could have found his way around without such a light.

And what was Armand doing in the library anyway? He had not struck me as a particularly bookish fellow, and none of the books were out when he was found. I will grant that sometimes there is pleasure to be had in simply sitting on a stool and looking at the rows and rows of beautiful bindings, but that is a joy to people like me, not normally associated with the likes of Armand, and certainly not in the dark.

The bell rang and I decided to go to Compline, on the grounds that I needed all the help I could get, so it would do no harm to ingratiate myself with Almighty God. The candlelight was soothing and soporific, not to mention the gentle rise and fall of the chanting. I found myself gazing upon the great silver crucifix borne in during the procession and uttering a prayer to the figure of Christ on it.

Come on, Lord. Help me out!

CHAPTER THIRTEEN

I lay on my bed, unable to sleep.

Normally, I sleep without any difficulty. I have had a lot of practice. As I get older, I get better at it. But on this particular evening, blessed oblivion eluded me.

This was partly due to a little voice inside my head telling me that if I only had three days to sort this out before people started to demand to be allowed to go home (for people, read a bishop) then I could ill afford to waste time in slumber.

On the other hand, I would not be the first person to remark that sometimes when I face an intractable problem I go to bed and the answer somehow comes to me during the night. On this particular night the only nocturnal thought thus far was that eating Limburger cheese within a week of bedtime was a very big mistake. You would need the innards of a goat to digest that stuff, except that feeding it to a goat would probably be considered as cruelty to an animal.

It was not just that I could not resolve this conundrum satisfactorily, nor even that I did not really know where to start. I was running around trying to look like I knew what I was doing when in my heart I knew that I did not. What made it worse was that other people took my frantic activity to be an indication of competence, and I could not imagine what they would say when I admitted failure on Sunday. It would not be so bad with many of them whom I would never see again, but I would have to travel back to Leiden with Senguerdius telling me repeatedly that I had let my beloved University down or, even worse, being horribly understanding about it.

And there was something else. You know that feeling that you have seen something of importance but you have no idea what it is? That the answer is staring you in the face, but you are too dim to see it? If not, try looking over my shoulder at my undergraduates' faces the next time I explain the concept of God's sanctifying grace to them. Anyway, I was feeling exactly that as I lay there in the dark.

Considering that we were in a city, the night was noisy. There was a tumult raised by some cats, then a period of silence, possibly connected with the arrival of a fox that barked a few times; then, just as I was dropping with sheer exhaustion, a nightingale began singing his disgustingly cheerful song. That brought the cats back.

I climbed out of bed to check that the window was closed and rapped my shin against the corner of my chest. [No, Van der Meer, don't be ridiculous. I don't mean the area of my ribs and breastbone. I mean the large box holding my effects.] I hope that Abbess Mathilde did not hear what I said, either then, or when I realised that my shin was bleeding. I struck a light for my candle, an act which always looks so easy when anybody else does it, and inspected the wound. It was not especially deep, but it had scraped the top layer of skin to one side and blood was running down to my ankle.

I found a kerchief, soaked it in the water on my nightstand, and pressed it against the wound as my grandmother had taught me to do many years before. I am not ashamed to say that I would have welcomed my grandmother's comforting embrace just at that moment. When I was a boy any problem seemed easier when I was held close to that capacious bosom, so long as I managed to keep my nose free so I could breathe. *If only she were here now*, I thought, before dismissing the idea on the grounds that she had been dead over six years and I would not really enjoy cuddling up to her given that fact.

After a while the bleeding stopped and I lay back to sleep, only to hear the kitchen springing into life, followed, inevitably, by the sound of people getting up to ready themselves for the first service of the day at six o'clock.

I shaved and dressed and stumbled down to the chapel.

'Good morning, Mercurius,' Senguerdius said cheerily. 'You look like you haven't slept for a week.'

'I haven't slept for a night,' I replied grumpily. 'Didn't you hear the cats? And the fox? And the nightingale?'

'Not a thing,' Senguerdius answered. 'Slept like a log.'

This intelligence did nothing to elevate my mood. Why is it that when you tell people you slept poorly they insist on telling you how well they slept, as if some unwritten law requires them to rub salt in your wound?

Since I was running out of clean hose I had put another kerchief over my wound to protect my clothes and proposed to speak to Gerlach after the service to get it properly dressed. It was no longer bleeding, though it smarted from time to time.

At the end of each service Brother Ambrose normally collected the valuable items from the chapel and returned them to the treasury, replacing them with more workaday alternatives. Since the gates were locked the Prior had decreed that this was not necessary, which left Brother Ambrose looking rather lost as we rose to go to breakfast. He did not know what to do with himself. As we left he stayed in his place looking confused and rather pitiful. He was not a young man, and I suppose those moments of cloudy thought come to us all in time. Fortunately I have been spared them thus far. [I could have sworn Van der Meer said something just then but he assures me that he did not.]

Despite the tragedy that had befallen us, Van Espen and Govarts were rigorously maintaining a separation from the Leiden team, presumably in the hope that we would soon resume the debate, a prospect that Senguerdius occasionally mentioned with relish, convinced as he was that a mighty victory awaited us. For a fleeting moment the idea crossed my mind that if I could not prove human hands were behind Armand's passing this was an argument in favour of their case. Indeed, I thought (unworthily, I admit) that they might have engineered the death for that very reason. Armand had not been much of a witness when alive, but dead he spoke potently about the power of witchcraft.

As I sat eating my breakfast I pulled a sheet of paper from my sleeve. On it I had written the names of all those who were known to be in the building when Armand met his end:

Bishop Johann Heinrich von Anethan, Chair of the judging panel — would probably think nothing of killing someone whom he thought deserved it, but he wouldn't do it himself. He would get a servant to do it.

Abbess Mathilde — clearly innocent.

Ehrenfried Walther von Tschirnhaus — not the most nimble man I had ever met. I could not imagine the old student sneaking up on anyone.

Dr Jakob Pfeiffer — away with the fairies much of the time. He was too busy copying inscriptions to waste precious minutes killing a witchfinder.

The three judges nominated by Leuven — they spent so much time talking to each other that they probably had not realised that Armand had been killed. Actually, I had not seen one of them move for some time. He was so gaunt and pale that it would not have surprised me if we had a second corpse on our hands soon. I made a note to myself to find out more about these three, because I had been ignoring them in my cogitations.

Wolferdus Senguerdius — if he turned his hand to homicide, he would no doubt be very good at it, as he was very good at everything else he tried. He would not have left a bleeding corpse to die in its own time. And if anyone was clever enough to get out of a locked room, it would be my Rector. Against that, what possible motive could he have? And I was fairly sure that I had seen him in the hall after supper on the fatal night. I suppose it would only have taken a minute or two to rush out and kill Armand.

Zeger Bernhard van Espen and Petrus Govarts — laying aside one's natural animosity towards one's opponents, and the fact that I thought Van Espen was a bit of a know-all to whom I did not really warm, why would either of them kill their one and only witness?

I almost forgot the Bishop's Chaplain. Von Anethan was attended by a long streak of fastidious misery called Augustus Hasselbach. Augustus was the second son of a noble family and therefore had to earn his own crust, so his relatives condemned him to a life of celibacy as a trade-off for feeding him. To judge by his appearance it was a bad deal. He did not look like he had eaten a square meal in his life, except for the lemon he must have been sucking to give him that sour expression.

Hasselbach, like most bishop's chaplains, spent much of his time as a mobile coat-rack, holding copes, mitres, gloves and similar things. I noticed that he always gave the chalice a quick polish before his master had to drink from it at the Eucharist, at which he spent much of his time saying Amen loudly after his master spoke and tutting over the state of the altar linen. No doubt his family hoped that one day he would himself be a dignitary of the church, and indeed he was. It took him until he was seventy-two, when he was appointed Archdeacon and promptly died. I discounted him as the murderer because he was always in the company of the bishop, and because entering the library would have required him to touch the door handle, which might have been held briefly by someone with dirty hands before him.

Then we came to the resident Brothers. I had been given a list compiled by Brother Theodemar. There was the Prior. It was not impossible that he had been moved to kill Armand, but the motivation would have had to be very strong, because he had been so upset that this had happened under his supervision.

Gerlach had access to all sorts of poisons, so why resort to hitting someone with a big stick of some kind?

Gilbert, the librarian, was a gentle soul, as librarians tend to be. When did you last hear of a murderous librarian? I suppose if Armand had bent back the corner of a page as a bookmark or flexed the spine to breaking point Gilbert might have been incensed, but beyond glowering at him and perhaps shushing in a marked manner, I could not imagine Gilbert taking much action.

I had not had much to do with Nathaniel and Andrew, who worked in the kitchen garden. They would have access to a range of tools, I suppose, and the strength to wield them effectively. I decided I must watch those two more closely.

As for Lodewijk, the cook, why resort to a blunt instrument when he had an array of wickedly sharp knives at his disposal? And we keep coming back to the lack of an obvious motive.

The same considerations applied to Theodemar, the guestmaster, Simon, the almoner and Ambrose, the treasurer. Unless and until I could show that they had a reason to kill

Armand, I could get nowhere. After that, I would have to work out how they could have done it and then escaped through a locked door, but compared with finding a motive, that might be the easy part.

I pushed the remains of my breakfast away, then felt guilty about wasting food and pulled my platter back to force down a piece of bread and some ham. The thought came to me that there was an added complication with the Brothers because they had gone off to the last prayers of the day and I did not think I had seen any after that, but I had seen Armand later. Knowing that they would be praying again at six in the morning I could imagine all the good little Brothers would be asleep in their beds when Armand was last seen alive.

Senguerdius patted me on the shoulder. 'Cheer up! It may never happen!'

'It already has,' I grumbled.

'Oh, you're thinking about poor Armand again.'

Who else would I have been thinking about? This whole affair looked likely to give me a fever on the brain, which might be injurious to my health. Back at the University just the previous winter Master Hubertus had narrowly escaped death when thinking hard about a knotty problem in mathematics. Admittedly that was because the large slate on which he wrote his workings fell off the wall when he was writing vigorously but it was only the piles of books and papers he never tidied away that meant the slate could not reach the floor and crush him beneath.

'Well, Mercurius,' Senguerdius pronounced, 'a trouble shared is a trouble halved. Let's hear your line of thinking.'

He sat beside me and clearly had no intention of leaving until I said something.

'The list of names I have gives me twenty suspects. Twenty-one, if I include myself, though I need hardly say that I did not kill him.'

'Neither did I,' Senguerdius said, 'so you can cross me off.'

'Forgive me, Rector, but if I go around crossing names off just because someone says that they did not do it then I'm going to run out of suspects fairly quickly.'

'That's true,' Senguerdius conceded, 'but if I'm staying on the list so are you, because I could say the same thing.'

I wrote my name on the list, but in very small writing.

'But I have no reason to accuse any one of these people. I can't think what the motive could be.'

Senguerdius pondered a moment. 'That's unscientific,' he finally decided.

'Unscientific?'

'Yes. You're positing that your acceptance of a fact depends upon your knowing why the fact is true. But that's unscientific. Think of my balloons.'

It took me a minute to realise what he was talking about.

'Oh, those paper things from the East!'

'That's right. I can't think why they fly upwards when you put a candle inside them. I've no doubt I'll work out the reason given a little leisure and access to my instruments at Leiden, but for now I don't know why they do that. However, I cannot deny that they do. I've seen it with my own eyes.'

'Your eyes might be deceiving you,' I suggested. We philosophers regularly trot that one out. The unreliability of our sense-experience is a favourite argument in the circles that I move in.

'They might, but unless there is a mass illusion that would have to be true of all the people who came to my demonstration in March. I didn't see you there, by the way.'

'Ah. No. I think I had a prior appointment.'

'Never mind. The point is that a large number of people saw the balloon fly away with the candle inside. Who knows how far it might have risen if the candle had not tipped over and burned the balloon to cinders? And let me add that some of those who saw this were undergraduates who frankly haven't the imagination to make up an illusion like that.'

I suddenly warmed to Senguerdius. It was good to know that I was not the only one who felt that way. 'I concede your point,' I said, unhappily.

'Motive would be good if one presented itself, but until it does, you must look at who could have had the opportunity. If we could find the weapon, that would be even better, but I fear that none exists, because it should have been in the locked room with Armand.'

'That's another thing,' I moaned. 'Armand was in a locked room. How did anyone kill him there?'

We sat in silence for a while because neither of us had an answer.

'Was the fire burning?' Senguerdius suddenly asked.

'The fire?'

'In the fireplace. Could someone have burned the weapon?'

I became very excited by this possibility, only to realise a problem. 'But they will have set new fires since. Whatever was in the ashes will be long gone.'

'They must be somewhere, Mercurius. If there were metal pieces in the ashes surely someone would have noticed.'

'I thought you searched the fireplace and chimney,' I said.

'I did.'

'And you found nothing.'

'But I was looking for an intact weapon, not one that had been reduced to ashes. Anyway, have you got a better idea?'

This idea of a weapon that disappears appealed to me.

'Could he had been struck with a large piece of ice that melted overnight?' I asked.

Senguerdius snorted. 'First, where would the killer get a large piece of ice at this time of year? Second, the ice would become water, and the floor was not wet.'

'Ah, indeed.'

Senguerdius tried another tack. 'Mercurius, let us lay aside the means, and wrestle with the opportunity.'

'But we have no way of knowing who was lurking in the shadows in the library.'

'No,' conceded Senguerdius, 'but that's not the question. Why kill him then?'

'The opportunity arose,' I stammered.

'But all the people on that list of yours could have killed him before Tuesday evening. Why did they kill him then?'

I was doubting that this would get us anywhere when an idea split my brain like a flash of lightning. 'He was going home!'

'I'm sorry?'

'Rector, you told everyone in the hall that we would ask him any questions first thing on Wednesday, then he could go home. If they were going to kill him, their hand was forced. They had to do it between the end of the debate on Tuesday afternoon and his departure on Wednesday.'

'And they could not rely on having an opportunity on Wednesday between our releasing him and his departure,' Senguerdius added. 'Mercurius, I think you may be right! Of course, I can't see how that helps us.'

'Well, it would rule out Brother Andrew and Brother Nathaniel, because they were not in the hall when you said it.'

'Yes, but someone may have told them at supper.'

I was not exactly crestfallen, but my crest was certainly wobbling a bit.

It was very slender, but perhaps it was a start. If someone had a reason to kill Armand, they had to do it on Tuesday evening.

We sat in uncompanionable silence for quite a while before I had another of my ideas, and a rather better one this time, even if I do say so myself.

'He said something,' I blurted out suddenly.

'Said something? Armand, you mean?'

'Yes. Something changed between morning and evening on Tuesday that meant he wasn't worth killing in the morning, but he was by evening. I can only think that he said something that someone did not like.'

'But what could that be?' Senguerdius asked.

'We'll have to review what he said,' I argued. 'How did he begin his evidence?'

'I don't know,' said Senguerdius. 'I wasn't listening.'

'Not listening? But he was a key witness.'

'A key witness for the other side, Mercurius,' Senguerdius emphasised. 'I wasn't going to repeat anything he said. It only reminds the jury of it, which would be a capital error in a debate.'

'An error if it was a telling point against us, Rector, but what if it was piffle?'

'Well, of course it was piffle, Mercurius. Everything the man said was piffle. There are no such things as witches. We know that.'

'But it doesn't matter what we think. It's the jury that counts. I thought I saw you recording his words so that you could attack his credibility.'

'Certainly not!' Senguerdius said huffily. 'You can do that on the last day if you want, but I have more than enough material of my own to fill the eight hours I'm allowed. I can't waste time repeating the spoutings of idiots.'

He said this in a way that seemed to be unashamedly directed at me, but I resolved not to allow my feelings to be hurt. Not too much, anyway.

'I didn't take a note either,' I admitted. 'I wonder if anyone did.'

'Govarts was writing furiously. Ask him.'

I will confess that I would sooner have eaten another plate of Limburger cheese than asked Govarts for help in the normal run of things. I had not warmed to him; but in the circumstances I had little choice, so I thanked the Rector for his assistance (if any) and headed out to look for Govarts.

CHAPTER FOURTEEN

Govarts was in the library, scribbling as fast as he could while marking a place in a book with his index finger. He appeared to be trying to write out the entire volume and, to judge by the pile of paper at his elbow, he was making good progress. *The papermakers of Leuven must be going through something of a boom time*, I thought.

'May I disturb you?' I asked.

'You already have,' he replied, continuing to write for a while before putting the pen down and flexing his fingers a few times to ease the cramp in his hand. 'But no matter. I am sure that a fellow scholar would not do so without good cause.'

He smiled. Somehow it made me feel like Eve must have done in the Garden of Eden when she saw the serpent coming towards her.

'Certainly I would not,' I assured him. It was true, too. There are few things as vexing to me as someone who insists on talking to me while I am trying to read. Since I am having a grumble let me add that I strongly deprecate the novel practice of writing learned treatises in languages other than Latin. Latin is, and always will be, the language of scholarship. I sometimes suspect that these reprobates eschew the ancient tongue because they do not have a mastery of it.

'I wonder if you are able to assist me?' I began soothingly. I often find that a request for help disarms the fractious person and wins his co-operation.

'If I can, I will, of course.'

'Thank you. That is most kind of you.'

That was enough of the unction. You can overdo these things if you are not careful.

'It is possible that Armand was killed because of something he said,' I added, before reflecting that I ought not to have told Govarts that in case he was the murderer.

'Indeed, Dr Mercurius? You intrigue me. Pray continue. What was it that he said?'

'I don't know. I was hoping that you might.'

Govarts' eyes opened wide. 'Why me?'

'We observed that you were taking more detailed notes than we were.'

'I took some notes, but by no means a verbatim record.'

'Do you still have them?'

'Yes, in my chamber.'

I breathed a sigh of relief. 'May I see them?'

Govarts took an age to reply. I began to suspect that he was searching for an unpleasant way to say no to me.

'We are both gentlemen, are we not?' he finally said.

I am. I don't know about you, I thought, but I nodded anyway.

'You will forgive any directness on my part, but we must be clear where we stand. Have I your word that you will not use anything that you see in my notes to gain an advantage when the debate resumes?'

It had not occurred to me that there was any possibility that the debate would resume. It was now Thursday, and von Anethan had declared his intention of going home on Sunday. Even if I solved the crime that very day, that would not fit that timetable. Senguerdius would have to speak on Friday, Govarts on Saturday, then we would be engaged in worship all day Sunday so I could not speak until Monday. Allowing the judges time to deliberate would take us into Tuesday. However, if the debate was unlikely to resume there was no reason not to give the assurance he was seeking, so I did so.

'May I also take it that anything you see in my papers will remain confidential, since I do not have time to edit or correct them?'

I had no idea what he could possibly mean, but he seemed to want me to say yes, so I did. He pondered for a moment, then rose from his stool.

'If you will have the goodness to wait here and guard my work I will go to my chamber and bring the papers to you. Then you can examine them here, if that is agreeable, and there will be no danger that any might be mislaid.'

He looked at me like a schoolmaster dealing with a boy whom he suspects of throwing acorns across the schoolroom — which, of course, I never did. It just rankles that one of my classmates saved his own skin by implicating me, which led to a very unpleasant interview with the master and a subsequent experience which my bottom did not enjoy. It would not have surprised me if Govarts had produced a leather strap at that minute as a warning.

'That is perfectly agreeable,' I uttered hoarsely. My mouth was unaccountably dry and I could somehow feel some stinging about my lower half.

'I shall return,' Govarts assured me. I just hoped he wasn't the murderer gone to fetch the instrument of death because I had somehow stumbled upon the proof of his guilt; though if that was the case, I had no idea what that proof could be. How unsatisfactory it would be if the murderer dispatched me because I was about to pin the blame on him when actually I had not the slightest idea who had done it. That would have been so unfair. I could only hope that for my own satisfaction I would see the murderer's face as he attacked me so that I would have a brief time to work out what had occurred in that library.

Govarts marched into the library with such vigour that I may have flinched upon seeing him in anticipation of a murderous attack.

'Don't worry,' he said cheerfully. 'I'm not the killer. Though I suppose I would say that even if I were, so the utility of such a comment is doubtful.'

That was one way of putting it, I suppose.

'I'm afraid these aren't very detailed,' Govarts continued, thrusting a bundle of papers into my hand. Goodness knows how much detail he would have liked to include, for there was so thick a wad given to me that it was hard to imagine what could have been omitted, especially given Van Espen's penchant for thinking hard before he said anything, leading to quite a bit of silence.

I suddenly realised that Govarts was standing over me and coughing gently.

'I'm terribly sorry,' I said. 'You'll want your stool back.'

'If you please. There are others at the end there.'

He tilted his head to indicate the farthest part of the room. Despite it being the middle of the day and Govarts having a candle on his desk, I could make out very little in the distant gloom. Anyone coming into the library for the first time would hardly know there was a wall there.

I picked up the papers, thanked Govarts again and promised to return them as soon as possible, before finding a desk and stool along one wall. I then had to disturb him again to ask where he had found his candle, and once more to ask if I might light mine from his. All I can say is that he was a man lacking in Christian patience.

I began to read Govarts' notes, which were models of their kind. There was some abbreviation and he had attempted to capture only the substance of a question or answer, not necessarily the words spoken, though sometimes those were easy to work out. For example, the very first exchange ran:

Q. Where he was born, and when.

A. Near Osnabrück, in the year of Our Lord 1627.

Q. The occupation of his father, and what family he had.

A. A dealer in wood. Took trees from the forest and prepared them as planks or boards before selling them. Five children of whom three lived to adulthood.

Q. When and how he came to be a witch-hunter.

A. He was apprenticed to one in 1640. Or apprenticed himself, his parents being dead and he having none to take charge of him. Had heard stories of the witch trials in Osnabrück forty years before his birth and many women executed, thus the scourge of witchcraft extirpated; but the threat renewed about that time, and the local witch-hunter being very old and feeble and desirous of passing on the craft to another.

Q. Whether he is married and hath family.

A. He married the only daughter of the said witch-hunter in 1646. Two children, both deceased as infants, and his wife dying too at that time of a distemper after childbirth. His sister lives yet, keeping a farm near to Osnabrück, and having two sons.

Q. His first work as a witch-hunter on his own account.

A. Hired by a group of citizens of Hagen after a mysterious fire in a metal-smelting factory caused much damage. Was able to prove that the fire was started maliciously by a woman at the behest of two men dismissed from the factory for drunkenness at work. Though she had been at home at the time that the fire started, yet he showed that she had sent bats to carry fire into the factory roof, causing it to burn down.

Q. Whether she was fairly tried and justly condemned.

A. Yes, by the magistrates, and burned, after which no more fires occurred, further proof of her guilt in the matter.

I started at the callousness of this. I know little about bats, but the idea that anyone could organise them to do anything was laughable. They would live in the roof because that is what bats do. As for the fire, it seemed to me much more likely that the drunken workmen had started it themselves, then blamed her when it all went wrong. Of course, I was not in the court at Hagen and I might be mistaken, but now that I thought back to Armand giving evidence during the debate it was quite clear that he believed all this guff, and was in earnest about the wickedness of the poor woman.

I returned to Govarts' notes.

Q. His later career.
A. There being no future in resting in a place once all witches and warlocks were detected, he became an itinerant witch-finder. He has regularly travelled throughout the German lands as far south as Trier, and to the east as far as Braunschweig. His repute being such that he is able to demand large fees as well as his expenses, and lives well.
Q. Will not ask his fees, but how are they set?
A. A daily rate, with his living, and a bonus upon successful completion. The bonus always paid, for he never fails.

This too was chilling. I suspected that he never failed because he had an interest in pinning something on anyone so long as he could gain a conviction and hence earn his bonus. It would be very hard for anyone accused of witchcraft to prove their innocence. After all, people allege witchcraft when they can find no rational explanation for an event; and the only way a person once accused can exonerate themselves is by finding such a rational explanation, in which endeavour others have already failed. The number of people accused of witchcraft who somehow managed to be acquitted must have been extremely small.

That was supposing you were lucky enough to have a conventional trial. Some of these women had been tried by ordeal, often by ducking in water. One hand was tied to the opposing foot and then they were thrown into a pond. If they floated, this showed that they had been rejected by the water, and hence were guilty. If they sank, they were innocent. They were also often dead, but at least they had died innocent and could therefore anticipate entry into Paradise. The astute reader will gather that I am sceptical about the value of this practice. To me, it seems like a rather unpleasant display of humiliating power over defenceless women who should have men's protection, but I suppose that as a lifelong bachelor I may not have been exposed to whatever evil women can do.

The next few questions were directed to learning how Armand identified women as witches. He referred several times to the book *Malleus Maleficarum*. I have skimmed this book, or at least the first few chapters, and have no hesitation in declaring it the biggest collection of half-baked ideas I have ever seen, with the possible exception of a student's essay on St Augustine of Hippo which lacked the magisterial sweep of *Malleus Maleficarum* but made up for that by plumbing astonishing depths of imbecility.

It was allegedly written by a Dominican called Kramer two hundred years ago, partly in response to being ordered to leave the Diocese of Brixen by the Bishop who had reservations about Kramer's methods and cockeyed theories and who described him as senile and crazy. There was also some criticism that Kramer was altogether too keen to ask witches about their intimate activities, that he jumped to conclusions without good evidence, and that he did not know the Catholic Church's teaching on demonology.

One of the most laughable chapters of *Malleus Maleficarum* describes how witches can mysteriously hide a man's virile member so that he can no longer see or feel it. It gives two examples, in one of which the young man so affected allegedly went to the tavern to cheer himself up by drinking wine, began talking to a woman and upon her asking why he was so downcast, immediately dropped his breeches and showed her the site of his misfortune, as if any man would open his thoughts to a strange woman and act in this way. (I will allow that Fat Lysbeth has probably seen the members of most of the students in Leiden, but only in her professional capacity, and she would certainly expect a handsome tip for rectifying any deficiency.)

[Van der Meer has just told me a most improbable tale concerning a friend of a friend of his who suffered a terrible accident, and all I can say is that anyone who puts any part of their body anywhere near a pig's mouth deserves whatever follows.]

Anyway, Armand seems to have considered that this book was a serious guide to the detection of witches, and Van Espen did nothing to dispute this, though I remembered that when Armand had claimed that the University of Cologne had approved the text Van Espen quickly changed the subject, which had not prevented von Anethan commenting drily that Kramer's document from the University was undoubtedly forged, and not particularly well forged at that. I had noticed Abbess Mathilde smiling gently at that remark, which might explain why I had completely missed the exchange that followed.

Q. His proudest achievement in his work.

A. His work in Bilstein some years ago, by which nine witches were detected, despite the unchristian doubts of the lord there, who sought to stop the process and thereby protect the said witches.

Q. The fate of the witches?

A. All burned alive, except a girl child of eight years who was sent to a convent due to her youth.

The gloating cruelty of the man was evident on the page. I was glad that the distraction had caused me to miss this vile boast.

Q. Does he still find work?

A. Less than in previous years, trade being good and general prosperity, for in good times there is less incentive to use the black arts for gain. But still consulted in cases of personal spite. Last year witness travelled to Bavaria at the request of a mayor whose wife was declining, she presently dying and upon being opened a foul black mass found in her bowels, but the woman whom the mayor suspected was able to say the Lord's Prayer and hold a Holy Bible against her bare skin without ill effect and was therefore judged innocent, though privately witness believes that she was guilty and the Devil by some secret work enabled her to endure the trials without ill effect.

If I understood this argument correctly, Armand was holding that there were ordeals which would prove whether a supposed witch was guilty or innocent, these being time-honoured and attested to in that wretched *Malleus Maleficarum* of his and similar volumes, and if the woman failed the ordeal, she was clearly guilty; but if she passed it, she was still guilty because the Devil must have helped her to go through the ordeal and thus faked her innocence. Goodness me, even Jesuits would not stoop to such an argument. Well, actually one or two might, but I am confident that the generality would not.

Q. Whether witness intends to retire soon.
A. Yes, for he tires of the travelling and would like to settle, perhaps buying an inn for the better sort of traveller. He might give thought to marrying again, though he retained happy memories of his Agatha. He might write his memoirs to occupy himself.

At least we have been spared that, one good thing to come out of his untimely death, I thought, then chastised myself for lack of Christian charity. Armand may have been a horrible, cruel and vindictive man, but he was still entitled to have his murder investigated. Yet when I read the notes again, I could see no reason for the Devil to worry about him, since he was a poor investigator who looked for scapegoats rather than the guilty. If there are real witches in the world, they had no more reason to fear Armand than they had to fear me.

My stomach began to grumble, and I suddenly realised that I was alone in the library. I went in search of some food and found the company already at dinner. Fortunately the Prior saw me enter and ordered some food to be brought for me, since they had made short work of much on the table.

'A successful day?' Senguerdius asked as I sat down beside him.

'I am no wiser,' I admitted. 'All I have learned is that I was not concentrating as I ought to have done when Armand was giving evidence.'

'You and me both,' Senguerdius replied. 'I couldn't decide whether to be bored or appalled by the man.'

'Did you notice any reaction to anything he said?'

Senguerdius pursed his lips and thought hard. 'To be honest, I think everyone thought the way I did,' he said at length. 'Abbess Mathilde shook her head when he said that women were more likely to succumb to the Devil's blandishments because they were less constant in the faith, which hardly surprised me. If you ask me he was quite brave to even mention that possibility in front of her. Oh, and von Anethan was animated about the suggestion that the University at Cologne had approved that stupid book Armand was prattling about. That reminds me, Mercurius, when we get back to Leiden I must get someone to go through the archives to see that the University hasn't approved anything like that.'

I could not imagine that we had. Trying to get anything published there subjected the author to a rigorous questioning before it was approved. Obviously these memoirs are not published by the University, or they would probably still be going through the system to this day.

'Nothing else?' I asked.

'I can't bring it to mind, but I'll keep thinking.'

It was disappointing that the two people he had singled out were the two I thought least likely to be guilty, myself excluded, of course.

There are times when getting blind drunk seems much the most rational course of action open to a man.

CHAPTER FIFTEEN

Once in a while I wonder if I still have the brains I was born with. [Van der Meer, that was not an invitation for you to make any comment. And stop smirking.]

Since I was completely without any idea who had killed Armand, or how they had managed to do it through a locked door, I decided the best thing to do was to ask Almighty God for help. He had not been keen to involve Himself in my enquiries in the past, but frankly I had no better idea and it is what we priests tell other people to do, so we should do it ourselves.

I resorted to the chapel and fell upon my knees, glancing about me to see that no-one was in sight before crossing myself and beginning to mumble a prayer. It was then that I noticed a figure in the shadows.

Brother Ambrose was polishing the vessels used for the Holy Eucharist. He was oblivious to my presence, so far as I could tell, and busy about his own prayers as he polished. I have no idea how much time he devoted to polishing but all the metal in sight was gleaming. The candlesticks, the crucifix on the altar, the processional cross…

That was the point at which my stupidity struck home. How could I have been so blind?

I rushed to the front before realising that this was extraordinarily undignified behaviour in a chapel, and the clatter of my feet must have disturbed Ambrose, who started.

'Master! What are you doing?'

'This cross! It's not the one that was here when we arrived.'

Ambrose looked thoroughly ashamed, as if I had caught him pawning the church's treasures to redeem his gambling debts. 'Ah. I had hoped...'

'I saw that the other day but I didn't take notice,' I continued, as much to chastise myself as to enlighten Ambrose. 'Why would you carry a silver crucifix in procession when all the rest of the metal here is gold?'

'Gilded rather than gold for the most part,' lamented Ambrose. 'If only we could afford a set such as befits Our Lord's majesty.'

'Gilded or gold,' I pressed him, 'where is the gold crucifix?'

'I have locked it away until the gates are opened and I can take it for repair,' he answered sadly.

'What happened to it?'

'I don't know, Master,' the poor Brother wailed. 'I cannot have stowed it correctly after a service and somehow it has become bent.'

'May I see it?

The unhappy fellow could hardly refuse me though he blushed mightily at the thought of showing so imperfect a sacred item to a visitor. He led me to a small door and unlocked it using a key attached to his belt by a chain.

'That key never leaves you?' I asked.

'Never, Master.'

'But there must be others?'

'The Prior has one, of course. I know of no others.'

Pushing the door open he invited me to step inside. There was barely room for the two of us, and it was very dark, the result of having no windows. Ambrose placed his candle on a small ledge by the door.

'I'm surprised you can find anything at all in here,' I said, as much to make him feel more at ease as with any expectation of response.

'I know where everything is, Master. I can find it without a candle. That's why I don't understand about the crucifix. See, it fits here, with its shaft in the bracket. Yet I couldn't find it on Wednesday morning, and when I came back with a candle after the service it was leaning against the wall. I had to use the silver one for Wednesday's service.'

'So you did. I remember now.'

Ambrose produced the crucifix and we took it into the light. The shaft was straight, but the cross at the top was bent slightly to one side — the left, as you looked at it.

'Have you cleaned it?' I asked.

'I haven't, I'm afraid.' Ambrose reddened again. 'Please don't tell the Prior, Master. I love this work and I should hate to lose the privilege of handling the Holy Vessels.'

'On the contrary, Brother Ambrose, you have done well. I need a stronger light. May I take this to an outer door?'

Ambrose led me through passageways to the garden. Fortunately the sun was shining, something which can never be taken for granted in my country, even in summer.

I sat on a stone and cradled the crucifix in my hands, tilting it to catch the light. As I suspected, there was something by Our Lord's feet.

'What do you see here, Brother?'

Ambrose peered at the figure on the cross and gasped. 'A miracle! Our Lord's wounds are bleeding afresh.'

'Not quite. It isn't his blood. It's Armand's. This is the weapon that was used to strike the fatal blows.'

'Blasphemy!' shrieked Ambrose, then, realising that this was ambiguous he added, 'Not you, Master. Whoever used it in such a way.'

Now that I had the instrument in my hands I could understand that strange wound on Armand's head. The horizontal arm of the cross had missed the head, so the main blow had been made by the portion of the cross beneath it. Seen in cross-section, it had a flat back but the figure of Christ on the front gave that a less defined shape. That was why the wound had one straight edge and one wavy edge.

'The killer must have grabbed this from the chapel. When was it unlocked?'

'After the gates were locked on Tuesday, Master. I would normally put the more valuable pieces away after the first morning service and replace them with the cheaper ones, which is why I was puzzled. It was not in its place.'

'But you said nothing?'

Ambrose bowed his head. His face reddened again and for a while he remained silent, then he began to cry quietly.

'What is it, Brother?' I asked.

'I feared that the honour would be taken from me if the loss was discovered, Master. It was foolish pride on my part. But I love this chapel and my work here.' The poor fellow raised his face towards me and showed an expression of the deepest anguish. 'I am not afraid of hard work, but I am not well suited to it. I hope I show my diligence in the polishing and care I give to the items in my charge. But I am not a young man and I know that some have been whispering in the Prior's ear that I am forgetful and vague. I hope that I am not, but I know my powers are diminishing. You will learn one day, Master, how terrible it is to know that a mind that was once sound is beginning to fail you.'

By God's good grace, I have not yet had to face this awful fate. [What was that, Van der Meer? Did you say something?]

'Who says these things?' I asked, hotly.

'I believe Theodemar has said so. And maybe Simon.'

'I see no sign of it,' I declared, crossing my fingers behind my back. There are occasions when God will forgive a little bending of the truth in a good cause.

'You are kind to say so,' Ambrose answered, forcing a weak smile. I just hoped he was not going to quote me to the Prior as some kind of reference for his continued ability.

I put my arm round his shoulder and patted him benevolently. 'Come now, bear up, for I believe you have given me the first sliver of light in this matter.'

'You know who killed Armand?'

'Well, no…'

'You know how it was done in a locked room?'

'Again, no…'

'Then I fail to see…'

'Come, Brother. I need you to lock this away again and do not let anyone have it without the Prior's permission. I will explain this to him. And, God willing, you will be able to take this blessed item for repair very soon.'

I do not know whether it was ever repaired. It would have taken a deal of skill, for it was quite severely bent. Precious metals, though heavy and beautiful, deform easily. Now that I looked at it again I could see that Our Lord's right knee was twisted towards the centre. Ambrose brightened and did as he was bidden, and I thanked him and went on my way.

The Prior listened carefully.

'I do not doubt what you tell me,' he said, rubbing his chin in thought, 'but I am surprised that there is any man so steeped in sin that he would use so precious an object to kill his fellow man.'

'I suspect that his anger was such that he gave no thought at all to what he was grabbing.'

'Such evil has been visited upon us!' sighed the Prior bitterly. I think he was regretting having agreed to host the debate, despite the money. If the truth be told, even the money was probably insufficient, given the amount we were eating and drinking. With little else to do, the jurors were making the most of their meals. Even Senguerdius, who was by no means a toper or glutton, was rarely seen without a cup of wine and some biscuits by his side.

'I should be grateful,' I said, 'if no mention was made of this discovery. If the murderer believes I am still floundering he may relax his guard.'

'And if he thinks you are on his track then he may decide he can only hang once however many he kills,' the Prior commented acerbically, as if a concern for my own safety was the real reason for my request. It would have been, if I had thought of that. 'How are your enquiries advanced by this?' the Prior continued. 'Do you know who wielded this weapon?'

'Not exactly,' I said.

'Not exactly? But you have an idea?'

'No.'

'And does it help you to understand how a man can be killed in a room where the door is locked from the inside?'

Why was everybody making such a big thing about that?

'No. Not one bit.'

The Prior resumed his seat and rested his chin on his hands as if in prayer.

'Oh, dear,' he said.

I chose not to take Senguerdius into my confidence. I had no reason to doubt his ability to keep a secret, but I had already said too much. There was no need for him to know, therefore I did not tell him. Besides which, this litany of questions from all quarters about my progress was becoming tiresome.

What had I discovered? No more than was ordinarily found at the scene of the crime. If Armand's body had been found with a dagger sticking out of his back nobody would have applauded me for identifying the cause of death. Finding the weapon now only put us in the position we would normally be in immediately after finding the body.

It also drew attention to another question I would have to answer. Not only had the murderer managed to kill someone within a locked room, but they had also somehow managed to retrieve the weapon and put it back in Ambrose's small inner treasury. On the other hand, the fact that it had only been returned some time later suggested a human agent rather than a supernatural one. Whoever it was had taken it away to remove the blood, because it was inconceivable that those traces I had found were all that had escaped from Armand's shattered skull.

I absentmindedly drank a beaker of ale while I was thinking about this; that is to say, I did not savour it, and had no recollection of draining the beaker, so deep was my thought.

Let us suppose that I had been the murderer. I know it is unlikely, but humour me a while. I have just been seized with a mighty passion and have struck down the unfortunate Armand. Let us leave aside all questions to do with how I got into the library through the locked door for the moment. Maybe it is possible to turn a key on the inside by means of a loop of thread passed through the keyhole from the outside. I must experiment.

Now I find myself with a bloodstained and damaged crucifix in my hands. If anyone sees me with it, and sees Armand's body, even the greatest fool in Christendom is going to jump to a conclusion and it is hard to see what innocent explanation I could possibly give. I might try saying a big boy did it and ran away; or that Armand did it himself and I have merely picked up the weapon; but neither of these propositions stands much chance of being believed. Surely with so much blood shed from Armand's scalp I must be spattered too. I need to get to some place where I can clean myself and the weapon in some privacy. No problem there, though; so far as I know everyone in the buildings has their own little room, and presumably they all have a jug of water there just as I (as Mercurius, not as the murderer) have.

The chances are that the Brothers have to empty and refill their own pitchers. We guests are privileged in that respect. But as a guest, how do I tip the bloodstained water away without drawing attention to myself? Whoever is sent to do it for me expects to empty a jug of water. If it is full of blood, they will notice; and they will notice too if my jug is empty because I have discarded the bloodstained water myself. I could try saying that I was thirsty during the night, I suppose, but few are gullible enough to fall for that.

That might point the finger at one of the Brothers. Certainly the circumstances of the death must exonerate Abbess Mathilde who surely could not employ a sacred object with such violence. I say that not solely because it was holy, but mainly because it was very heavy. A crucifix on a staff taller than a man and fashioned from gold and silver is no trifle.

So why not return the crucifix before it is missed? The killer was taking a great chance in holding on to it one minute longer than necessary, therefore it must have been necessary.

Unaccountably my beaker was empty again. I looked on the floor in case I had spilt it but there was no sign of the contents. Now, where was I?

Ah, yes — why keep the crucifix so that it was not available on Wednesday? Maybe he was trying to straighten the top so that no questions would be asked about it. He could not have known that Brother Ambrose would keep quiet about the damage for his own reasons, unless, of course, he was one of those who had been insinuating that the poor treasurer was unfit for his office.

I ought not to overlook the possibility that Ambrose was responsible for the death of Armand and had concocted the story that he had told me to obscure his guilt. It seemed unlikely, but over the years I have seen a number of unlikely criminals, and an even greater number of highly suspicious and detestable men who turned out to be innocent, at least of the crime alleged against them.

That blood on the crucifix intrigued me. There had not been a deal of it, just some lodged against the nails that pierced Christ's hands and feet, but surely there must once have been much more given the depth and width of the wound. So the killer had cleaned the crucifix but had missed small amounts. If he was going to clean it, why not do a thorough job? He might as well have left it by the body instead of spiriting it away through the locked door and taking it to clean, running the risk of being found with it in his possession as a result.

It may be that he felt some remorse at using a sacred object for so evil a purpose and wanted to rectify matters as far as he could, though I am bound to say that Catholic and Reformed scholars would agree that when he stood before Almighty God on Judgment Day he would be questioned much more closely about killing a man in cold blood than about having a dirty crucifix.

The evening was drawing in, and I was conscious of having wasted the afternoon in idle speculation. Platters were being laid on the long tables and candles were lit and placed at both ends of each of them.

Candles! Of course. The killer would have to clean the crucifix by candlelight, and in this setting a candle burning late was more likely to attract notice from the other brothers. The light could be seen under the doors by anyone who passed. Even if this had not been so, each door had a small hatch that could be opened from the outside, so that the Prior could observe whatever was done within. If a Brother had done this, he would invite an inspection if his candle were still burning. The murderer would have needed daylight to be sure that he had cleaned the blood off the crucifix, and since the first service of the day was around dawn, he would have no chance to return the crucifix before then. Ambrose was absentminded enough to assume that if there were no processional cross he must have forgotten to put one out. I had seen him looking confused that Wednesday morning but had not thought anything of it.

Presumably the murderer had, as he thought, cleaned all the blood off and wanted to return the cross as soon as may be, so he had returned it at the first opportunity. It was pure guesswork on my part, but since he could have bumped into anyone on the way I assume he moved the cross close to the time of a service in the chapel, when a Brother with a processional cross would not have looked out of place.

Senguerdius nudged me with his elbow. The Prior was about to say Grace before dinner and had been waiting patiently for me to bow my head. I mouthed an apology and did so.

'You seem pensive, Mercurius. May I know what you are thinking?' Senguerdius enquired.

'I am thinking that I can now picture a sequence of events.'

'So you know how the murder was committed behind a locked door?'

'No.'

'Perhaps, then, you know the murderer?'

'No. But I have excluded some from consideration.'

'Oh. May I ask whom?'

'Abbess Mathilde.'

'I understand, Mercurius.'

'No, you don't. It's not because she's a woman. Well, actually it is. But it's because the killing required more physical strength than a woman has.'

'We've been through this, Mercurius.'

'Yes, Rector.'

'If you've seen a woman throw her clog at her husband you might reconsider your view.'

'And the rest of the judges,' I added. 'I don't think they did it either. But I can't tell you why just yet.'

'So you think it's one of the Brothers?'

'Possibly.'

'Possibly? Mercurius, if it isn't a judge, and it's not you or me, surely it must be one of the Brothers.'

'Well…' I began.

'Van Espen! I knew it! Or possibly Govarts. Disappointment at the quality of Armand's evidence I'll be bound.'

It was not worth trying to have an argument about it. I let him think that while I had something to eat.

CHAPTER SIXTEEN

Thursdays are altogether too close to Sundays, I decided, and Thursday nights are depressingly on the eve of Sunday.

I sat on my bed with just a flickering of my little candle for illumination. And that mirrored the interior of my brain, where the last gutterings of any idea were bravely trying to stay alight in the face of all-encompassing darkness.

Things had reached such a pass that the best idea I could come up with was to say a prayer and then open my Bible in the hope that the Almighty would finally pull his finger out. I know that God has fingers because I have seen a copy of Michelangelo's painting on the ceiling of the Sistine Chapel where He is reaching out to Adam. It was shown to me by a student who wished to know whether Adam should have had a navel.

I knelt in prayer then let my Bible fall open, which it did at Luke's Gospel, chapter 24. This was no surprise, because a book will generally fall open where it has been most often read, and this is one of the places where the story of the Resurrection of Our Lord is told. The women come to anoint his body and find it has gone. Two men in shining clothes say to them 'Why seek you the living with the dead? He is not here…'

Well, I thought, *a fat lot of help that was.*

I lay down on my bed and blew out the candle, said another couple of prayers, and tried to snatch a little sleep before the nightingales, foxes and tomcats began the impromptu concert in the early morning.

Needless to say, almost immediately a cat began wailing. I was looking for something that I could throw at it when an idea came to me. Could the weapon have been thrown at Armand? Or dropped, perhaps?

I resolved to look at the roof of the library to see if there was a beam the murderer might have sat on while we entered, because we had been looking at ground level. Could he have hidden there, waited until we had all gone, then dropped to the ground and escaped?

Friday dawned, far too early for my liking, and I reluctantly left my bed to inspect the library once more. The cats of Maastricht have quite astonishing vocal stamina, though lacking something in harmony and, indeed, melody. Even as I shaved they were still calling to each other responsorially. In the grim night hours I fancied I had made some headway in learning a cat vocabulary and could interpret some of their dialogues.

'This is my rooftop.'

'That is what you think.'

'This is my rooftop, I say, and I lay claim to that lady cat.'

'That is what you think.'

'Go no closer to her, or you will be sorry.'

'That is what you think.'

A fight ensues.

'I told you that you would be sorry.'

'I am not sorry. I will defy you from a distance. And I have just urinated on your territory to make a point.'

A combination of tiredness, pressure of expectation and fear of failure was weighing heavily upon me. My mind was not at its best, not helped by Senguerdius and his eternal optimism.

'Maybe today, eh, Mercurius?'

'What about today, Rector?'

'Maybe you will find the killer today. I have every confidence in you. Try this ham, it's remarkably good.'

I could not, of course, since it was Friday and I was a secret Catholic. I was rather surprised to see it on the table at all, since only two or three people there could eat it, but perhaps the Brothers put it there as a temptation to make their foregoing of it more of an act of self-denial, in the same way as I have heard of holy men who invite women to their beds so that they can ignore them all night as a demonstration of their celibacy.

Moodily, I grabbed a piece of the loaf and plastered it in butter. It was an untoward indulgence, but I needed some spoiling in the circumstances.

'Have you made any headway?' Senguerdius enquired.

Since he had seen me at dinner the night before and I had slept — at least, gone to my bed — in the intervening period, I do not know what progress he could reasonably have expected. The Stadhouder was notorious for working along the same lines. William would send an ambassador to some foreign land, and no sooner had they arrived than a messenger from The Hague would turn up with a letter asking how things were going.

'None whatsoever,' I admitted.

'Never mind,' said Senguerdius chirpily, 'it's only a matter of time, I'm sure.'

I wondered if you could be dismissed for belabouring a University Rector over the head with an oak platter. (I have checked; there is no precedent.)

I was not going to tell him, but even my nocturnal inspiration had been wrecked by the discovery that the library ceiling was all too visible and nobody taller than a man's knee could possibly have crouched up there. Wherever the murderer had concealed himself, it had not been there.

I took a mouthful of drink and found it to be water rather than beer. Maybe that was the Brothers' regular Friday privation?

All in all, this investigation was going so badly I had half a mind to stand up on Sunday and announce that it was indeed the Devil's work, no human agent being involved, and do so with all the panache and certainty I could muster in the hope that my reputation would not be damaged by my abject failure.

On top of all else, Brother Ambrose approached me once more to beg me not to reveal his derelictions to the Prior while assuring me that he was truly penitent. He, like me, had gone without much sleep that night, but whereas I had been kept awake by amorous wildlife, Ambrose had been kneeling in his cell scourging himself with a little whip and praying fervently. I am all for contrition and confession but I see no reason why God cannot wait until daylight, since day and night are all one to Him (Psalm 138:12 by the Catholic reckoning, more or less).

I assured Ambrose that when I undertake that I will say nothing, I will keep my word, and grasped his shoulder in a friendly and supportive way, causing him to yelp piteously because I had forgotten about the scourging.

'You should let Brother Gerlach give you some salve for that,' I suggested.

'The pain is part of the penance, Master, and must be endured,' the unhappy man replied.

'A penance you have laid upon your own shoulders,' I answered, before realising that this was not, perhaps, the most felicitous phrase I could have used. 'I mean that he who imposes a penance can lessen it where there is need. You have confessed your sin and made satisfaction for it. God is compassionate and will forgive you for seeking help so that you can attend better to your duties.'

Ambrose's eyes filled with tears, so much so that I checked my hands were not causing him pain again. 'You are very compassionate, Master. I thank you. But I can bear the suffering so long as my service as Treasurer is allowed to continue. Dismissal would smart more than any amount of scourging.'

I might have disputed whether that was literally true, but it seemed neither the time nor the place, so I excused myself and went off to find a piece of wall somewhere that I could bang my head against until I had a new idea.

I walked along the narrow passage that led from the treasury past the library to the chapel deep in thought. The treasury and library doors were on the same side of the corridor, then I turned the corner and walked along what I supposed to be the outer wall of the library. I had not paused to think about the floor plan of the place. The corridor was quite long but if the murderer had somehow left the library this is the way he must have gone. Turning right out of the library door would have led to the treasury and then the Prior's office; I was unsure what lay beyond the next bend. However, turning left out of the library would lead him into a corridor too narrow to allow anyone coming the other way to pass easily. The thought came to me that I should look for any sign that a human killer had fled that way.

There were no niches or particularly dark corners. There was painted glass in the windows to my right such that nobody could see in unless, I imagined, there had been lights in the corridor. I walked slowly along, inspecting the walls and floor with no great hope of a breakthrough, largely for want of any better way to employ my time.

I was about halfway along the corridor when something caught my eye. In a crevice in the floor there was a stain, reddish-brown rather than red, but I had seen such stains when my father killed an animal. I was sure it was blood. There was not much, but there was some.

I stepped back and tried looking at the floor from a range of angles. There was nothing to be seen. But that was the surprising thing. The floor was very clean; so much so that I formed the opinion that it had been recently swabbed. Not all of it, of course, but a patch about a pace across and two paces front to back.

I squatted on my haunches and tried to make sense of this, and my memory dredged up the Bible reading of the night before. 'He is not here.'

Oh, Mercurius, you complete fool!

The mystery of the murder inside the locked library was no mystery at all. If there was nobody in the room but Armand then Armand must have locked the door himself; and he did so to keep a murderer out.

I could see it quite clearly in my mind's eye. He must have been walking along the corridor with his back to the chapel. The attacker struck and Armand, unable to defend himself against so fierce an assault, had run for his life. With barely a couple of paces' start his only advantage was that the killer was carrying a heavy processional cross, but when he reached the library he must have seen the door open and the key in the lock, exactly as had been described by Brother Gilbert. He had grabbed the key and slammed the door shut, locking it behind him. But what then?

He was wounded, grievously so, though perhaps he did not know it. He would retreat from the door in case the assailant could get through it. He would check that there was no other way in, for I doubted that Armand had been in the library before. The safest place would be in the middle of the room where we found him. If he had cried out, nobody had heard. His attacker would be keen to finish the job, but could hardly risk waiting outside the door with the bloody weapon in his hands. He must have taken it to hide and clean it, trusting that the blows he had landed would be sufficient to kill Armand; and so they had proved. After some little time — a minute, half an hour, who knew? — Armand had slumped to the floor and died.

How had I been so puzzled for so long? I could only think that it was because I had been persuaded by the general opinion that the murder must have been committed in a locked room because the victim was in a locked room. But if the victim locked it himself there was no mystery about that at all. We had not found blood in the corridor because we had not looked for it, being so certain that we knew what must have happened.

Now that I had begun to pull on the thread of the mystery more was becoming clearer with each minute. The cap was under Armand's body because he had pulled it off to assess how bad his wound was. Before that the cap had acted like the pad I had applied to my leg when I cut it, serving to hold at least some of the flow back by pressing on the wound; but when he pulled it off it could flow freely. It would not surprise me if the sudden eruption of blood caused him to feel faint and fall to the floor where he presently died.

Everything was finally revealed to me. Well, not quite everything. I still had no idea who the killer was.

I prowled the corridor outside the library door in the hope, admittedly an illogical one, that some kind of trace of the killer had been left hanging in the air to guide me towards an accusation. It was Friday, so I still had two days to find that out, and I could see two ways of doing so.

I could carry on as I was and walk around looking bewildered. *People must be quite used to that by now*, I thought, but the killer might betray himself, or I might think of some way of identifying him.

Alternatively, I could announce all that I had discovered, give the impression that I was on the killer's trail, and panic him into some hasty action that disclosed his identity. It could work if he believed me. He might flee, thus confirming his guilt.

On the other hand, he might call my bluff. There was only so long that I could go around looking confident. Eventually I would have to admit that I did not know who it was.

Even worse, the desperate act he might take in his panic might be to silence me before I could name him. I cherished hopes that I would die at a great age, peacefully, in my bed; I still have, to be honest. The prospect of my brains being spattered along a corridor of a church in Maastricht did not appeal. Maybe I could hint that someone else knew the answer in the hope that he would attack them first? No, that would be unbecoming and cowardly, not to mention being extremely unlikely to fool anyone who had any wits at all. Since the killer was not one of my undergraduates I discarded that idea.

I wanted to keep all this information to myself for now, but I needed the help of others to bring the matter to a proper conclusion, so I thought very hard about a key question: who was best placed to give me the help I needed?

Senguerdius was loyal and intelligent, but knew nobody there except me. I doubted what effectual help he could possibly give me.

Abbess Mathilde was also intelligent, and I judged her to be shrewd and a good judge of character, but the same deficiency applied.

Von Anethan was keen to put this whole sordid business behind him, and I was sure of his innocence if only because I doubted if a man dressed in all his finery could have freed his arms sufficiently to give anyone a blow with a processional cross, an act that he would undoubtedly have considered to be blasphemous. The trouble was that von Anethan expected to be obeyed, and I did not think he had the appetite for methodical consideration of the evidence that was needed here. He would have stood up and ordered the villain to confess at once or face excommunication and the eternal fires of Hell. Bishops can do that sort of thing, or at least those who would be affected by his rulings believed he could.

General excommunications of unknown malefactors were declared every so often when there was no other way to lay guilt at a villain's feet, and they often worked. All Catholics would be under a never-ending obligation to report anything relevant that they heard to von Anethan, the chief problem being that you could bet your last stijver that they would report a lot of irrelevant dross as well, if not instead. The poor fellow would soon be swamped by allegations of gaming, making the sign of the Cross with the wrong hand, gluttony, sexual impropriety and eating meat on a Friday. Eventually, if all went to plan, the miscreant would own up and von Anethan could then hear his confession, reconcile him to the Church and spare him all those little demons with red-hot pincers that we read so much about. After all, eternal life is all very well, but most of us who are chasing after it hope we will be spending it in Paradise; it becomes a lot less appealing if you are heading for the other place; and who would know that better than one of the brothers here? Just think of the embarrassment when all your colleagues are in Heaven and one of them remarks 'Has anyone seen Brother X lately? He's definitely dead — I'd have thought he would be here by now.'

I badly needed some beer. Half an hour in Steen's Inn and I was sure my brain would be restored to its best. I was not made for fine wine, good food (which I define as anything not cooked by Albrecht) or gracious living, though I will admit that the feather mattress I bought myself a while ago is a wonderful thing for an old man with sore hips. [Van der Meer believes that this infirmity will spare him the kick up the backside I occasionally threaten. It will not. Even though it pains me more than him, I would chastise him if necessary.]

Glancing out of an open window I chanced to see Abbess Mathilde sitting on a bench in the garden reading her prayers. Her linen was, as always, spotless, and she sat with a back that was effortlessly straight and tall. Amid all the grief and turmoil she alone seemed serene and imperturbable, sailing through the storm like a mighty ship.

I do not mind saying that I was entranced. Forget any vulgar assumptions that may be crossing your minds; it was her state of peace that I envied. Perhaps if I could cultivate that for a while it would clear my head and allow me to focus?

I found my way to the garden and waited for a moment so as not to disturb her. Quietly I stepped over to another bench and sat there, trying to empty my mind so that I could begin meditating on something other than the murder of poor Armand. I took my little New Testament from my pouch and opened it at the First Epistle of St Paul to Timothy, always a favourite of mine. However, by the time I reached the ninth verse with its catalogue of murderers of fathers, mothers and others I decided I had made a bad choice.

I glanced up and jumped with surprise. Abbess Mathilde was drinking from a cup brought to her by a young nun. I had had no idea that there were any other nuns in the buildings, and my confusion was increased when I saw Abbess Mathilde point in my direction and the young nun walked towards me to offer me a cup of cold water from her pitcher. I could not refuse so gracious a gift, and thanked them both, at which the young woman cast her eyes downwards and said nothing. She bowed her head and walked away from me, pausing in front of Mathilde for her blessing, after which they exchanged a couple of sentences in German and the young woman returned to the building behind the Abbess.

Of course, a woman could hardly travel alone, even in the company of churchmen, and I felt stupid that I had not realised before that Abbess Mathilde would have an attendant. There may be womanly needs that could not be met by a manservant or the brothers; and once they had arrived the young woman would be instructed to remain in their quarters all day, meals being taken to her. It must have been a lonely trip, but someone would have to undertake it for the safety and comfort of their beloved Abbess (though I pity any footpad who attempted to take liberties with Mathilde).

A gnawing thought would not leave me. If I had not noticed a nun about the place, what else had I not seen?

CHAPTER SEVENTEEN

I sat at the table feeling rather anti-social. I was in no mood for polite conversation, even in Latin, and I could not escape the sensation that everyone was looking at me, including the murderer.

Feeling that you are in the same room as a killer is not a comfortable experience, though I suppose that after a few days I should have been getting used to it. Things were not helped in the chapel earlier during the introit when someone walked past me with the processional cross and I flinched violently, causing Theodemar to ask if I was quite all right. I had to cure myself of that reaction. It would be rather inconvenient to go through life as a priest crouching and covering your head with your arms whenever anyone walks towards you with a large cross.

Maastricht being far from the sea, the fish offered at dinner were river fish. Let us not beat about the bush; they were eels. I do not mind eels, but Abbess Mathilde did not eat them, and contented herself with bread and cheese, followed by some fruit.

'You seem not to have much of an appetite tonight, Master,' she said. 'Do you not eat eels either?'

'I do, but I am not very hungry.'

'I realise that you Protestants are probably used to meat despite it being a Friday. I appreciate your willingness to follow our custom.'

I smiled at the undeserved compliment. We were not eating meat because nobody had given us meat. I eat what is placed in front of me — except that, as a secret Catholic, I sometimes have to be cunning in avoiding eating meat on Fridays without drawing attention to the fact that I am not eating meat on Fridays. At Leiden I can usually get away with saying that the meat is burnt, because it always is, Albrecht taking the view that well-done is just a starting point when it comes to cooking meat. Of course, this does not explain why I eat it on other days, when it is equally charred. There was one memorable occasion when a kitchen boy let the fire die down and the meat appeared to be perfectly cooked, but Albrecht insisted on holding up dinner for twenty minutes until he had incinerated it properly. Seen in that light, not having meat on our plates saved me the effort of counterfeiting a reason for not eating it.

Von Anethan asked politely if I expected to conclude matters before he left, to which I replied that I was making every effort to do so, without adding that I thought he was a heartless and unreasonable beast for instructing me to fall in with his timetable. It was then that he removed the last vestiges of my appetite by asking the Prior a question.

'Is all arranged for the Solemn Funeral Mass tomorrow?'

I do not know why I was so shocked. I suppose I had assumed that somehow Armand's body was going to be returned to his family for burial. It was the third day after he had died, something which brought to mind things that had happened to someone else on the third day, as we recite whenever we say the Creed, and usually people are buried before then, especially in the summer heat. I had naïvely assumed that the brothers had got on with burying him somewhere with a private ceremony. It had not occurred to me that he might still be in the crypt or some similar place.

'We are prepared, Your Grace. If you will say the Mass I will act as your Deacon.'

'Excellent. I think for those of us who fast before receiving the Blessed Sacrament it would be convenient to begin early. Shall we say eight o'clock?'

I restrained myself from blurting out, 'And what about those of us who need a good breakfast before facing the day?' I had not got much of an appetite, it was true, but choosing not to eat and being compelled not to eat are very different things.

I ought not to think on an empty stomach because the ideas I have then are rarely my best. On this particular Friday evening I came up with one of the daftest of my life. I cannot think what came over me. I would attribute it to the promptings of the Evil One, if I believed in that sort of thing.

You see, there is a widespread belief among the country folk that if a murderer touches his victim's corpse it will spontaneously bleed, thus demonstrating his guilt. Whether that was given any credence in Maastricht or Germany, I did not know, but it seemed to me unimportant whether it was widely held so long as the murderer could be led to believe it.

'Your Grace, Father Prior,' I interrupted boldly, 'may I ask a question about the Mass? In my native area it is the custom for all present to file past and kiss the hand of the corpse to take our formal leave of him. Will that be done here?'

Von Anethan looked at me severely. 'I am not familiar with that custom.'

It was then that my guardian angel came to my aid.

'It sounds very fitting, I must say,' said Abbess Mathilde. 'For a man who was serving the Church by giving his time to be here, and who would, perhaps, still be alive if he had not done his duty, it seems a very proper mark of respect. It would not, of course, be expected of those who have the heavy duty of conducting the funeral rites,' she added quickly.

I like to think that she knew what was in my mind and decided to support me, but maybe she was just a thoughtful and considerate person.

'Well,' von Anethan pronounced after some thought, 'if it is a local custom I see no harm in it. And it would be a very appropriate gesture on the part of the Brothers here; if Father Prior has no objection, of course?'

Father Prior was trapped in a corner and looked at us like a fox cub that has seen the hounds coming. 'We will follow your direction, Your Grace,' he said.

All of a sudden my appetite had returned. Unfortunately the gannets round the table had already eaten all the choicest foods, but I selected a large piece of cheese, some bread and an indulgent chunk of their excellent butter, and tucked in.

Now I had him! In the morning the murderer would have to touch Armand's hand. My guess was that if the superstition was known there — and I would make it my business that evening to comment to as many as I could that this was common knowledge outside their cloisters — the murderer would do whatever he could to avoid actual contact. I supposed that he would kneel, move his lips towards the hand but not make any contact. All I had to do was to watch closely and all would be revealed.

The only alternative the murderer had was to flee during the hours of darkness, in which event his identity would be discovered and I could leave it to the local authorities to chase after him. This particularly appealed to me because I have never managed to reconcile myself to the capital punishment of men and women as a result of my enquiries, so I could tell myself that if he were subsequently trapped and sentenced it was not my doing. Learned men tell me that I am too sensitive on the point and that God in several places in the Bible ordains the death of a man, but they are not faced with the personal responsibility that I feel. I think that by this stage of my career four men had gone to meet their Maker as a result of my enquiries, and I regretted every one of them, albeit that they were wicked creatures to do what they had done.

Each time the jug came my way I filled my cup and thus went to bed content, replete and horribly self-satisfied. I would not need to reason any further, because on Saturday morning all would be brought into the bright light of day. Goodness, but I slept well!

Would that I still felt that way when I woke.

For some unknown reason I had chosen to lie with my head hanging over the edge of the bed, resulting in a terrible headache and rather a giddy feeling when I suddenly sat upright. This I did on the floor, having tumbled off the bed due to a misapprehension about which way was up.

The footsteps of people in the corridor outside seemed three times louder than usual, and my poor head was utterly unprepared for the sound of frantic hammering at my chamber door.

Before I had the chance to cover my ears with the pillow the latch was lifted and Brother Nathaniel, one of those who worked in the garden, charged in.

'Forgive me, Master! Father Prior asks that you come with all speed!'

He rushed out before I had the chance to ask where I was going and why I was needed, but I could scarcely argue with my host, so I splashed my face with cold water, shrugged my garments on and walked briskly towards the chapel, thinking that I must have overslept and missed the start of the funeral.

I walked through the door and my worst fears were realised; von Anethan, the Prior and all the brothers were formed up in a circle around the bier where Armand's body had been brought the previous evening in preparation for the Mass for the Dead. I began to formulate a suitable apology for my tardiness.

I then realised that they were incompletely robed. Von Anethan was a stickler for proper liturgical dress. He would surely never conduct a Requiem Mass without the necessary vestments. Looking around, I noticed that Abbess Mathilde was not there either. Perhaps she had overslept too.

I walked forward to take my place and the circle of brothers opened to admit me. I bowed to von Anethan and tried to look grave, as befitted the occasion. However, my composure was soon dispersed as I found myself asking the question they had already asked.

'Where is Armand's body?'

This was wretchedly inconvenient. When I conceived the plan on the previous evening, the response that I had not considered was that the murderer might dispose of the body to avoid having to touch it in front of us all.

'Is everyone accounted for?' I asked.

'Indeed we are,' replied Theodemar. 'Except the ladies, of course. And your Rector, Professor Senguerdius.'

Senguerdius? Could he be the killer? It seemed incredible. He was a man of great learning and, to that point, undisputed probity. Could he have deceived me so completely?

My mind was reeling at this unexpected turn of events when the man himself walked through the door and took in the empty bier.

'Am I too late?' he asked. 'Have you already buried him?'

The Prior explained what had happened.

'We brought him here before Vespers and stood vigil over him until midnight. He was here when we retired. But between then and six o'clock this morning he disappeared.'

Senguerdius showed no great emotion but leaned over to speak to me in a low voice. 'I suppose there's no doubt that he was actually dead?' he asked.

'I don't have a medical degree,' I replied, 'but when a man has a hole in his head, goes cold and doesn't move for three days I'd say it was pretty certain,' earning myself a look of some reproof.

'So it is unlikely that he simply took himself off,' Senguerdius reflected.

'Very. Apart from anything else, he hasn't got any clothes on.'

While I was still dithering, the Prior took charge.

'The outside gates are still locked. He must be in the grounds somewhere. We must search diligently for him before this becomes a matter of scandal.'

This aspect had not occurred to me before. A church does not want to gain a reputation as a place where your dead loved ones disappear.

The Prior was assigning areas of search to each of the Brothers, while I was feverishly trying to think of anywhere that I had seen where a body could be stored out of sight.

'Rector, have you seen anywhere that a body could be hidden?'

'Under the altar?'

We rushed to check but there was no possibility of hiding anything beneath the altar. Nor, indeed, could we see anywhere else in the chapel that would conceal anyone the size of Armand.

I was at a loss to know how to proceed when I noticed a young Brother enter. Despite his hurry he genuflected when he approached the altar, almost tripping over the hem of his habit as he did so, then continued towards me. He was a broad-shouldered youth with a haircut that looked as if it had been attempted with garden shears.

'Master, I am puzzled. This may be nothing, but I thought I should tell you. Or rather show you. If it's not too much trouble...'

'Lead on, Brother ... Andrew, isn't it?'

He smiled at being recognised. 'It is, Master. I work in the kitchen garden.'

That is where he led us, Senguerdius having decided that he did not want to miss this. Andrew warned us to watch our step as we went through the kitchen door, as if we were feeble-witted old men who would easily stumble, although I suppose when you are barely twenty a couple of men nearing fifty years old seem like Methuselahs.

He pointed at something by the wall. 'See what I mean, Master?'

'What exactly are you pointing at, Brother?'

'Our handcart, Master. We use it for moving heavy or bulky stuff around.'

I had gathered that much. I am not so cut off from worldly matters that I do not know the normal use of a cart.

'But it's the wrong way round, Master. Nathaniel and I always leave it with the shafts pointing outwards. Then if we need to bring in the donkey we don't have to try to turn the cart in this little paved area with the donkey in the way. I'm sure we left it last night just as we always do. But now it's side on, as you can see.'

I gazed up at the sky, earning myself a rebuke from Senguerdius.

'This is no time to admire the clouds, Mercurius. Surely this cart has been used to transport Armand's body.'

'Undoubtedly,' I said, 'but I was trying to gauge how dark this corner would be at night. Presumably the killer could not see to return the cart to its original place.'

Brother Andrew dropped to his knees to pick something from the ground. 'I think he tried, Master, but knocked this pot over. See, the side is cracked where it hit the wall.'

'That would make a noise, so he would run off and just leave it where it was. Thank you, Brother Andrew, this is most helpful.'

I began to look for tracks that we might follow. There was nothing on the paving, but when the path became beaten earth a fresh cart track could be seen. In a few places it was less visible, but it clearly led across the garden.

'Do you have a compost heap?' I asked.

'We do, Master, but it's the other way. The townsfolk wouldn't like the smell if it was near the outer wall.'

'So, Brother Andrew, do you have any idea where we are heading?'

Andrew scratched his head as his eyes swept from left to right and back again. 'There are sheds and outbuildings.'

We could see the other Brothers systematically working their way through these. If Armand was there, they would find him. But wherever we were going, surely the killer would be reliant on moonlight to find a hiding place. He would not dare to mount a lantern on the cart. It must be a place he knew well.

'Where do you get your water, Brother?'

Finding water is not a problem in most Dutch towns. We are surrounded by the stuff. If anything, the problem is keeping it out. Maastricht was slightly different though.

Many towns here are crossed by canals which brings water near to the houses, but Maastricht does not have so many of these. So far as I could see, the nearest one was a hundred or more paces from the church grounds; but, more to the point, if the Prior had been able to order the gates to be locked that implied there must be a source of water inside the compound.

'There's a well, Master, across the yard.'

We hastened to find it, and peered down into the dark hole.

'Can you see anything?' Senguerdius asked.

'Not a thing,' I replied. 'How deep is it?'

'Not very deep at all, Master. It doesn't need to be,' Andrew explained.

'And is there always water in it?'

'I've never known there not to be.'

'Could we find a light?'

Brother Andrew ran off and soon returned with a lantern attached to a length of rope. He began feeding it down into the well and slowly more came into view, but he had to stop when the lantern hit the surface of the water. Slowly he moved it from side to side so that the light penetrated new areas of gloom.

'There!' shouted Senguerdius.

I had already seen it. Poking out of the water was a bare foot.

CHAPTER EIGHTEEN

I need hardly explain that this was most vexing. My plan, already disturbed by the body scarpering during the night, was now dependent on raising Armand from the depths of a well, and I had no idea how to set about it. Well, I did, but I did not like the idea that I had.

Senguerdius, much to my surprise, had stepped onto the rim of the well and was yanking on the cross beam from which the bucket dangled.

'That seems pretty secure to me,' he announced. 'It'll take my weight without much problem.'

'Rector,' I said, 'should you really be clambering down a well? It's not very consistent with your dignity.'

'Never mind my dignity,' he replied, 'I'm not going down there. But if it takes my weight it'll easily take yours.'

'Me?'

At times of stress my voice shifts from manly baritone towards the alto register. At this particular moment I was nearer to a boy treble.

'Who else? As you point out, it's not dignified for me to do it. Brother Andrew won't fit alongside the bucket. And if you involve the other Brothers you are necessarily bringing in the murderer who may cut the rope as you go down. It's best if we sort this out ourselves and present the murderer with the retrieved body.'

To say I was doubtful understates my concern. Not so much doubtful as downright opposed, really, but there was some truth in his words. If we were able to do it ourselves it would be safer for me, and if I sent someone else down and the murderer cut the rope I would never forgive myself.

I began to strip off my outer garments. 'Brother Andrew, could you find me a suitable piece of rope? And if Brother Nathaniel is at hand it would be useful to have some extra strength at the top to haul me up.'

Andrew nodded and ran off to make the necessary arrangements.

'This is a brave thing you're doing, Mercurius,' Senguerdius told me. I did not want to hear that. If it was brave that must be because it involved peril, and I like a life free of peril. The only excitement I want is that of finding a new library.

Senguerdius was occupied in detaching the bucket from the rope. Having done so he looped it around my waist, between my legs, around my chest and under my armpit. He then yanked on it a couple of times which demonstrated that it was altogether too snug between my legs and I had to sit down for a minute to compose myself.

Andrew and Nathaniel returned and the rope that they brought was slipped under my belt so that I could not drop it entirely. They lowered the lantern again and I stood on the rim of the well.

'Right,' said Senguerdius. 'No point in hanging around.'

'Just a moment,' I said, 'if we're taking the bucket off doesn't that mean Brother Andrew would fit…'

'Off you go,' said Senguerdius, giving me a shove, and before I knew it I was dangling in mid-air and clinging to the rope that Andrew and Nathaniel were playing out altogether too quickly for my liking.

The lantern had been lowered ahead of me and tied to a peg by the side of the well so that the ropes could not become entangled. I descended towards the light, wondering again if this was what being born had been like, except that I did not come into the world feet first nor, so far as I know, were two gardeners controlling my speed of descent; if controlling is the word I want for what seemed to me to be recklessly fast.

Soon I could see the exposed foot and began trying to extricate the second rope from my belt using one hand, because I was determined to cling to my own rope with the other. It was quite difficult, but eventually I worked out that I needed to push it upwards because that was the reverse of the way it had gone in, and soon I had the loose end in my hand.

I cannot say that I was keen to touch Armand's corpse, but there was no other way to retrieve it, so I gingerly took his foot in my hand and threaded the rope around his ankle with the other. To do this I had to let go of my own rope, and was pleasantly surprised to find that I did not fall precipitately to my death, but stayed hanging in the air, unfortunately the wrong way round.

I jammed my feet against the wall and began walking round the well to turn myself. This was going very well until my foot lodged against some obstacle or other. I pulled to free it, and the obstacle moved.

'Could you send another lantern down?' I yelled. 'This one seems to have fallen off the rope.'

There was some muttering at the surface, from which I gathered that Senguerdius was going to take the strain on the rope while Brother Andrew went for the lantern.

Any amount of time seems longer when you are sitting in the dark, and the knowledge that I was sharing my space with a corpse did nothing to steady my nerves, but eventually I heard a cry of 'Look out below!' and a second lantern began its descent.

When it was in place I steeled my nerves and grasped the cold, wet foot again. I tied a firm knot and told them to begin hauling slowly.

'Not me! Pull Armand up!'

'If we're going to do that, Master, we will have to let go of you,' called Brother Andrew.

'Then whatever you do, don't pull Armand up!'

'Make your mind up, Mercurius,' snapped Senguerdius.

'How about if you pull us both up together?'

'I'm not sure we're strong enough for that,' Andrew said. 'Should I fetch some others?'

'Will you have to let go of the rope?'

'Yes.'

'Then don't! Ask Professor Senguerdius if he would be so kind.'

Senguerdius' face appeared over the rim of the well. 'I thought you didn't want the others to know what we were doing?' he called.

'No, I didn't. But I've changed my mind if it means I can come up.'

Senguerdius sighed. 'Have it your own way,' he said, and went off to find some others to help.

'We could raise you, Master,' Brother Andrew called.

'Thank you, but we really need to pull Armand free of the water so that we can get a rope on his other ankle.'

'I see,' said Andrew. 'But — forgive me, Master — we don't have another rope.'

'Then I'll loop this one round him somewhere so we don't risk pulling his leg off.'

I did not know if this was a genuine risk, but I did not want to take the chance.

'Help is here now, Master. What do you want us to do?' Andrew asked.

'Pull us both up slowly until Armand is clear of the surface. I'll shout when you must stop.'

I heard Senguerdius counting one, two, three and then there was a tug that took my breath away and I started to rise. I could see Armand coming out of the water, though his other leg was jammed behind his body.

'Stop!' I instructed. 'Can you wiggle Armand slightly to the right?'

'His right or our right?' asked Senguerdius.

I flung an arm out to my side. 'That way!'

I will allow that I was becoming rather fractious. It was cold and dark, and if I did not loosen one of these ropes soon I would be eligible for a nunnery.

They did as I asked and I leant forward and pulled Armand's leg free, which allowed me to work my way along it and grab the shin. I had no slack in the rope to carry out my original plan, so I decided all I could do was keep hold of it all the way to the surface, however unpleasant the thought.

'As before!' I called. 'Same speed.'

Senguerdius again counted one, two, three. I may have squealed as the rope was tightened.

Up we moved, a foot or two at a time. Eventually I felt the morning sun on my head and could see the brothers clustered around the well.

'Quick! Take hold of him before he falls!' ordered Senguerdius. 'No, not Mercurius! Armand!'

I am pleased to say that Andrew and Nathaniel took hold of me and hauled me over the rim of the well. I lay on the ground panting. I badly wanted to rub the numbness out of my groin but I thought my action might be misconstrued, so I just lay there and whimpered.

The Prior had arrived and was directing the Brothers. 'Let us cover his nakedness and do all things decently for this poor man. Andrew, Nathaniel, Theodemar, Gerlach, please bring something suitable and convey him to the chapel once again.'

'With respect, Father Prior,' Gerlach said, 'I think he should be washed again before we return him to the chapel. I could bring my herbs and lotions to the crypt if that would be more convenient.'

'A charitable thought, Brother Gerlach. Let it be done as you suggest.'

The party moved off, and I dragged myself to my feet.

'Thank you, Master,' said the Prior. 'I am ashamed that a guest of ours should have had to undergo such an ordeal here.'

I waved it away as if it was of no account.

'And that you should have had to descend to help him,' he added.

'It was necessary,' I replied. 'If you will excuse me, I will go and change my shirt.'

As I re-entered the building I was surprised to find the young nun waiting for me. She lowered her head so far that it was difficult to make out what she said.

'The Reverend Mother asked me to bring you this, Master.'

She held out a tray on which there was a cup of steaming liquid. I took a sip, and immediately experienced a feeling of warmth across my chest.

'It's very good,' I said. 'What is it?'

'Honeyed spiced wine,' said the young nun. 'The Abbess made it herself when she heard what was happening.'

'It is very kind of her. And you are kind to bring it. Have you been at the convent long?'

'I have never known any other home, Master. I was a foundling.'

I was rather taken aback. I had heard of foundlings of course, but I do not think I had met one before. When mothers are unable to provide for a newborn baby they are sometimes reduced to wrapping them in a blanket and leaving them at the door of a convent or beguinage to be reliant on the charity of the sisters there.

'I am sorry to hear it,' I said. 'And you have no family?'

'I know none,' she said. 'I am told I had a brother once. In fact, one of the Brothers here asked me if he might be my brother, for he had a sister once, but how would I know?'

'Which Brother was that?'

'I do not know his name, Master.'

'Could you point him out to me? If, for example, I brought you to supper this evening? With the Abbess's permission, of course.'

'I must be obedient,' she replied.

'What is your name, child?'

'Hildegard, Master.'

'Then thank you again, Hildegard. That was very restorative and just what I needed.'

She bobbed and left me to think. The Abbess was truly a remarkable woman. In other circumstances she would have made an excellent wife for some lucky man.

Not a man wearing a shirt as smelly as this, though, I reminded myself.

Von Anethan had been occupying himself all this while in doing what bishops do best, kneeling in prayer in the chapel, which is where I found him after I changed and washed myself.

'*Fidelium, Deus, omnium conditor et redemptor,*' he mumbled.

It is the start of a prayer beseeching God to remit the sins of his servants so that, by reverent prayers, they may obtain pardon. Armand was past doing any reverent praying, so it was important that we who remained did it for him.

'Dr Mercurius, I believe we are indebted to you for finding our poor Brother Armand.'

I could not think of any reply that would not sound conceited so I said nothing.

'Are you any closer to finding the culprit?'

'I have made some headway,' I answered. 'I have hopes that with the help of others I shall have an answer before you leave.'

'God be praised!' He wrapped a fatherly arm around my shoulders. 'It is a great shame that you are not a Catholic,' he said. 'Holy Mother Church has much need of competent young men as administrators.'

I smiled weakly. If only he knew.

I knelt in the chapel, ostensibly praying but doing so with an eye on Armand's freshly washed body to ensure no more underhand dealing with it. In any event, I felt in need of God's guidance to ensure that my plan did not miscarry.

An idea had come to me but it seemed so fantastic that I did not quite know how to test it. Fortunately I would have time to think during the Requiem Mass; plenty of time, if it lasted as long as some I have seen.

We had been offered wine and biscuits at midday but I declined. Wine and I do not seem to get along too well together, at least if I plan to get any work done, and I had already enjoyed Abbess Mathilde's artful mixture. While the others were partaking I remained kneeling by the body.

The door to the chapel opened and I heard cautious footsteps. Whoever it was must have seen me, because they quickened and ran away from me. That, I was fairly confident, had been the murderer, whose plan was now foiled, whatever it had been, but by the time I turned to look the door was swinging closed and I could not see anyone. They must be quite desperate not to have to kiss Armand's hand. Even if they were to creep up and kill me, they could not avoid discovery so long as Armand's body remained here. It would be scant consolation to me, I suppose, but I hoped that the killer was intelligent enough to realise the futility of a second murder. I would be busy over the next few hours, and I needed the help of the Prior, Hildegard and Senguerdius. I needed each of them to give me a name, and I hoped and believed that if I asked the right question I would get the same answer from each.

At one o'clock we were all assembled and the Requiem Mass for Friedrich Armand began. After about twenty minutes I was beginning to wish I had accepted the wine and biscuits, and by the time we reached the actual Eucharist I could have eaten all the wafers by myself, but I schooled myself to remain vigilant.

Von Anethan pronounced the Absolution and began that beautiful prayer 'May the angels lead thee into Paradise', at which the Brothers formed into a line and waited their turn to kiss the corpse's hand; but just as the first one stepped towards the bier, he stopped, for Abbess Mathilde had risen and was walking forward. She dropped to her knees with stunning elegance, bowed her head and kissed the hand. It was so simple, yet so graceful, I was quite overwhelmed.

As a result my eyes followed her as she continued around the bier and returned to her place, and I missed Brother Gilbert kissing the hand. Brother Gerlach was next, but to my horror when he knelt he placed himself between me and the hand. I tried to shift my position without making it too obvious that I was looking, so I managed to see Brother Ambrose kiss Armand's hand, but he left it dangling off the bier so I did not see the next two until Brother Andrew carefully restored it to its former position alongside the body for Brother Nathaniel to kiss.

I wondered briefly if anyone would think that I was a terrible person if I shouted out 'You'll have to do it again — I couldn't see,' or even 'No, the custom says you have to kiss both hands.'

One thing was very clear — the body had not started to bleed. But then I had never believed that it would.

It seems that a messenger could not be sent to Armand's family because nobody knew exactly where they were, except that it was somewhere near Osnabrück, so by gracious permission of the Prior, Armand was laid to rest as if he had been a Brother of the community. As we were walking away I managed to pluck Senguerdius' sleeve.

'Did you see who didn't kiss the hand?' I asked.

'I thought you were watching for that.'

'I was, but I couldn't see clearly. Gerlach knelt in front of me and Ambrose left the hand dangling out of my line of sight. I'd hoped that you might have seen from where you were.'

'I saw that Abbess Mathilde kissed it. My word, Mercurius, isn't she magnificent?'

'Yes, but…'

'I'll bet she runs that convent like clockwork.'

'Yes, but…'

'Quite a loss to our sex though. A woman like that could do anything; manage a household, bring up a man's children, run an estate…'

'Be a student at the University?'

'Don't be ridiculous, man. Though she would be an adornment,' he mused. 'I'll wager if she lectured we'd have no trouble getting the undergraduates to turn up, eh?'

I would not have wished our undergraduates on Armand, let alone Abbess Mathilde. They try my patience sometimes and I am the most patient man in Leiden. [What was that, Van der Meer? No, I'm sure you said something.]

'To return to my question, Rector, did you see any of the brothers fail to kiss the hand?'

'I'm afraid not. You'd need very sharp eyesight to be sure in that light, you know.'

I sighed with disappointment. All that clambering down the well had been for nothing.

'I'll tell you one thing, though,' Senguerdius continued.

'Yes?' I said hopefully.

'Well, if Brother Ambrose grabbed the hand, he can't be the murderer, can he?'

I did not feel that this observation had got us far, and nearly told him so. But I bit my lip.

Hard.

CHAPTER NINETEEN

Having had no joy from Senguerdius, it was time to speak to the Prior. I knocked at his door and he received me warmly.

'How may I be of assistance?' he asked, always a good start to a conversation.

'I wonder if you have any information about the antecedents of the Brothers here.'

'You think one of them has committed this terrible crime?'

I wanted to say no and reassure him but it would not have been truthful. It would also have removed any justification for looking at his records.

'I regret that I do, Father Prior.'

He stood and turned away from me as if looking out of the window, though all you could see was sky. 'I feared as much. One had only to realise the coincidence of timing. The killer could only be a Brother or a judge. And the judges are people of outstanding probity and good name.'

Not to mention most of them being too decrepit to lift a heavy processional cross, I thought, but said nothing.

He reached into his habit for a key which he used to open a small chest bolted to the floor by a broad iron band that climbed up each side and wrapped over the lip of the lower part. Reaching inside the chest he produced a book wrapped in a piece of blue cloth. 'The *Liber Status Animarum*,' he announced.

The Book of the State of Souls. I was not sure whether to take it or kiss it, he handled it with such reverence.

'I am sure that I can trust you not to reveal anything confidential that you may read here,' he continued. The fact that he needed to say it obviously demonstrated that he could not trust me or it could have gone unsaid.

'Of course. I would not ask if it were not necessary.'

'I know,' he said quietly. 'These days have aged me. I did not know such evil lurked within these hallowed precincts, and I cannot help wondering what signs I may have missed, what opportunities to deflect the wicked heart from so great a sin.'

'I think there were none,' I replied. 'If we had not been visited upon you, this could not have happened. I believe the killing was an impulse.'

'A very strong one!' exclaimed the Prior.

'Undoubtedly. But sometimes the waters of sin build up behind a dam, contained for many years, and then the dam breaks.'

'And all that pent-up power is released. Yes, I see the analogy.'

I asked his permission to sit at the other side of his desk and began to read the book. For each Brother, including those who had left, there was a page. It described when they came to the community and from where. Sometimes there was a next of kin given, though often not. It also listed any property they brought into the community so that, at least in theory, it could be returned to them if they left. For a few, there was the mention of 'a great sin confessed and absolution given' though without any details of it. Derelictions such as missing Mass were also recorded, as were gifts made after entry. A Brother had inherited a small farm which he donated, and the rents were listed as they were received. Finally, for many of the Brothers there was the phrase *Obiit* and a date. A few had moved to another community and one had been promoted to a high office in the church.

I found each of the Brothers in turn and looked for the detail I wanted. One by one Brothers were excluded until only two remained, and of these two, one was clearly the more likely culprit on the grounds of age. But this was hardly proof, just a circumstance that led me to suspicion. I needed more, but it was not to be found here.

I thanked the Prior and told him that I hoped that by the end of the afternoon I would have resolved the matter. There would be further pain to undergo, but the uncertainty would be dispelled once blame for Armand's death could be attributed to one man and only one. For a little while I had considered that more than one person might be involved, but I did not now need to postulate an accomplice. I could see what might have happened and why. I just needed to confirm it.

Abbess Mathilde was, as usual, reading. I think it was the same prayer book that she read and re-read throughout her stay unless she was an astonishingly slow reader.

'I hope you are recovered from your ordeal down the well,' she said with so warm a smile that I almost forgot that she was a nun.

'Much better, thank you. And thank you for that wonderful mixture.'

'I am glad that I was able to help, being prevented by my sex from playing any part in the recovery of Herr Armand's body.'

I found it hard to imagine this woman being prevented by her sex from doing anything that she wanted to do, but I knew what she meant.

'I wonder if I may ask you a question. And, of course, if anything was said to you in confidence I would not expect an answer.'

I meant that. There are those who would argue that anything said to a priest during Confession is confidential but that since women cannot be priests they cannot be allowed the same privilege; but I am sure that anything a nun says to her superior in the same circumstances must be treated the same way.

'Of course, Dr Mercurius. I will answer if I can.'

'I met your colleague for the first time earlier today.'

'Yes, I sent Hildegard to you.'

'She remarked that a Brother here asked if she might be his sister. Were you aware of that?'

'Yes, she told me.'

'Do you know which Brother it was?'

'I did not see him and Hildegard does not know his name. And, of course, she has been secluded from the Brothers while we have been here. One cannot be too careful. They may be religious, but they are still men.'

'Oh, indeed! As am I,' I added clumsily.

'I did not doubt it,' she replied with that mischievous smile again. 'But I think you may be trusted. And Hildegard is just next door.'

'I asked if she would be willing to identify the Brother concerned to me when we dine tonight, if you were kind enough to give permission.'

'I will give permission, of course; but please tell me first, do you suspect that Brother of the commission of Armand's murder?'

'I do. I think I know who it is, but I cannot prove it as yet. However, Hildegard's description of their conversation contains an element that fits with my hypothesis.'

Mathilde put her book down and rested her head on her folded hands for a few seconds while she thought. 'You will forgive my frankness on so serious a matter — it will not have escaped you that naming this man could be dangerous for Hildegard. How do I know that it will be safe for her to do so?'

'He will be detained at once.'

'How?'

I should probably have come up with a better answer than 'Eh?'. Without the mayors making their constables available — and why would they when they had not been informed of the killing — it was not easy to think how the Brother might be restrained.

'I am not entirely reassured, Dr Mercurius,' Mathilde continued.

'No. No, you wouldn't be. I will have Brothers Andrew and Nathaniel on hand to seize him, and I will guard Hildegard personally. An assailant will have to kill me to reach her.'

Mathilde appraised me carefully. 'I have seen, Dr Mercurius, how brave you can be. Not many men would descend a dark well with only a frayed rope connecting them to safety.'

Needless to say, if I had known that the rope was anything less than perfect I would not have descended on it, and I could feel my mouth turning quite dry as I thought of it. Senguerdius must have seen the rope and he had said nothing. How sorry he would have been if it had snapped and he had been forced to explain to the University authorities that he had lost one of their most gifted lecturers through such negligence.

'If I have your personal assurance that you will do everything in your power to keep Hildegard safe I will let her come with you.'

'You will be there too, I hope?'

'Oh, yes. I would not miss it. It promises to be most exciting.'

There remained an hour until dinner when I planned to confront the villain, before which I had some tasks to undertake. First things first; I found Andrew and Nathaniel and asked them to be prepared to restrain the man I named if he should become aggressive. They agreed, though not without some qualms on Nathaniel's part.

'We are committed to living without violence,' he explained.

I was struggling to compose some suitably accommodating answer to this objection when Andrew saved me the trouble.

'You can't subdue someone peacefully, Nathaniel. Have mercy on him by all means, but wait until he is lying on the floor with his hands tied.'

'Whom will we be subduing?' Nathaniel then asked.

'I can't tell you yet.'

'Is it a secret?'

'No. I don't know for sure who it is. I've narrowed it down to two.'

'What if you pick the wrong one?'

'If I'm not sure I won't say anything, and then you will not be called upon to subdue him.'

'But — forgive me — you might be sure, but wrong.'

I fixed him with the cold stare I reserve for argumentative undergraduates. 'I might be, but I won't be.'

I think I observed Andrew gently grab Nathaniel's arm as if to caution him to drop the subject.

'We will do as you ask, Master,' he said.

This filled me with confidence, because Andrew was easily the most muscular man there. Gerlach might have been bigger, but he was also flabbier. While Nathaniel was not large, his arms showed the effects of a lot of digging.

I next went to find Senguerdius to tell him what I had in mind. I told him whom I suspected and why, looking to him to find any flaw in my logic before I made a fool of myself.

'I can't fault your logic,' he said cheerfully, 'because so far as I can see there isn't any. Not formal logic anyway. You do have a credible chain of circumstances though, if that is what you are really asking.'

The reader will forgive my breaking off here for a moment for a short rant. I am a lecturer in moral philosophy and ethics at one of Europe's leading universities. (I would argue that it is *the* leading university, but let me be generous to the lesser ones for the time being.) I did not get that job, nor my Master's degree, nor my Doctorate, without knowing formal logic when I see it. Crimes are not solved by syllogisms. They are solved by painstaking gathering of information, ruthless cross-checking of facts, and high-quality inductive reasoning. Sometimes a bit of luck and an unexpected confession helps, I admit. But I knew what I was doing, and I was not convinced that Senguerdius acknowledged that.

The meal was a tense affair. The Brothers may not have been aware of it, but the leading men (and woman) knew what was afoot and they were waiting for me to say my piece.

I had made some notes to ensure that I did not forget anything, then forgot to bring them. No matter; I had read them over so many times I could picture all the words on the page.

I was just wondering how to interrupt the meal when the Prior stood up.

'I understand, Your Grace, that Dr Mercurius has some matters he wishes to lay before us.'

All eyes turned towards me, which was embarrassing because I had just taken a large bite from an apple. I tried to swallow it quickly and had a rather undignified coughing fit, relieved in some measure by a hearty slap on the back from Senguerdius.

'Thank you, Father Prior, Your Grace. You asked me to investigate the lamented death of Herr Armand, which I have done, and it is now time that I disclose what I believe to have happened. Since the gates here have been locked since the event it will come as no surprise to anyone that the killer is in this room.'

There was a satisfying little frisson of excitement from those present who were too dim to have realised that.

'You will recall that one of the great puzzles of this case was how Armand could have been murdered in a room locked from the inside. Clearly he could not have been. In fact, he was not killed there. He died there, it is true, but if the door was locked from the inside and he was the only person present then he must have locked it himself.'

This time I was rewarded with a gasp. This is one of the nicest features of dealing with religious brothers. They are so unworldly that many of them are surprised by the simplest things.

'No, Armand was attacked in the corridor that runs down the side of the library. I found blood there, though the killer had attempted to remove it by swabbing the floor. Since this had to be done in secrecy he had been forced to do so in the hours of darkness and with great speed. He removed what he could, but then had to hope that nobody would notice the small traces in the crevices of the floor.'

I took a sip of water to let that sink in and see if anyone was edging towards the door. The man I believed to be guilty was looking me steadily in the eye.

'The weapon used to perpetrate the attack was the golden processional cross from the chapel...'

'Gilded,' Brother Ambrose corrected me.

There was considerable hubbub after this revelation, quite a bit of crossing of oneself and general shock among the religious.

'Is the cross damaged?' asked the Prior, directing the question to Brother Ambrose.

'I am afraid it is bent,' I interjected, 'but please do not judge Brother Ambrose for not disclosing this to you. I asked him to keep matters secret until now so as not to alert the murderer to the fact that we had discovered this.'

Brother Ambrose looked mightily relieved; and if it was not strictly true it was a defensible half-truth, because I would have told him that if he had not already kept his mouth shut for his own reasons.

'The fact that anyone here would use so sacred an object for so profane a purpose leads me to think that it was not a cold-blooded or planned killing, but a matter of high passion for which there must have been an immediate cause.'

Senguerdius was nodding gently. I was glad to see that he approved of my deduction and that I was not devoid of logic after all.

'I next asked myself why Armand had been killed on that particular night. He had been here some days, so the killer might have done so at other times were he so minded. Of course, whatever the cause was might not have been triggered before then. But the passion of the attack implied that the cause was very recent, so I judged that it arose some time on Tuesday.'

I could see people around the hall working out the days on their fingers and asking themselves what they had been doing on Tuesday.

'You will recall that on Tuesday our colleagues from Leuven introduced their case. As part of this, Dr Van Espen called Armand as a witness, and he testified for some part of the day. We were, of course, entitled to cross-examine him as part of our reply on Wednesday, and Professor Senguerdius gave notice on our behalf that we did not expect to do so. Armand would therefore be going home on Wednesday; thus, if the killer intended any action, it would have to be on Tuesday night. That does not mean that the murder was premeditated. It seems more likely to me that the killer confronted Armand about some part of his evidence and, not receiving a satisfactory response, was moved to great anger and rash action.'

This was the point at which I began to wish that I had brought my notes, because everything was starting to get rather tangled in my head.

'It seemed clear that Armand must have said something during his testimony that had additional meaning for someone here. There are two ways to approach this. We could try to find something in his words that may have caused offence or distress, but that was difficult without knowing the person involved. I was indebted to Professor Govarts for his detailed notes of Armand's words, and with the help of the community's records I found a possible link.'

I was trying hard not to look at one man in particular lest he realised that I had divined his secret, but equally I must not avoid looking at him which would be just as much of a giveaway.

'At one point Dr Van Espen asked Armand to describe his proudest achievement, and he answered that he took particular pride in his work in Bilstein, where he detected nine witches. Eight of the witches were burned, but one small girl was sent to a convent. All that may well have been true, but he left someone out. And when I heard that someone here had been asking Abbess Mathilde's colleague Hildegard whether she once had a brother, the chain seemed complete to me. You see, Hildegard is not his sister, she is too young, and in any event she was not taken to her convent as an eight-year-old. But the fact that he had a sister who had been taken to a convent, and that he had evidently lost contact with her, gave me a motive.'

Out of the corner of my eye I could see Andrew swinging his legs clear of his bench so that he could move quickly if required. Nathaniel was sitting with a furrowed brow as if this was all too complicated for him. Perhaps it was.

'But I discovered that only two of the community here hail from the Bilstein area; and if the culprit could plausibly have Hildegard as a sister that rules out Brother Gerlach, who must be at least twenty years too old. And so we are left with just one.'

CHAPTER TWENTY

Everyone was agog, but I did not want to name my suspect yet, because I wanted to provide him with some mitigation. It did not excuse what he had done but it made it, perhaps, more understandable.

'I want to say a little, if you will indulge me, about Armand's account. He spoke of nine females, eight adults and one child. He did not mention that the child was the daughter of one of the adults. I do not know that, of course, but I suspect it. Nor did he mention that there was also a little boy, who, though utterly blameless when it came to witchcraft, was nonetheless grievously punished. For his mother and sister were taken from him, the mother burned to death and the sister taken to a convent, he knew not where. I imagine that something similar happened to him. Am I right, Brother Theodemar?'

Theodemar stood, but made no attempt to flee. Those near him edged away as if he might lash out at them, but he did not do so. Instead he began to address the company with an unsteady voice.

'I was barely twelve years old. My sister was actually seven, not quite eight. And I have never seen her again since that day when we were forced to watch our mother being burned. We were told she was a wicked and spiteful woman. She was not. We knew better. We knew she loved us. She was not worried about her fate for herself, but it broke her heart to know that she was leaving us to fend for ourselves. Our father had already died when we were very small.'

He faltered and tears flowed from his eyes which he wiped on his sleeve.

'Armand caused that — and he boasted about it! He said it was his finest hour. He wrecked more families than ours, I am sure, and it had to be stopped. I know I will pay dearly but I could do nothing else in honour of our mother's memory.'

He took a deep breath and tried to compose himself.

'I spoke to him after the session and asked if he would meet me that evening. He did not keep the appointment, so I lay in wait for him, loitering in the doorway of the chapel so I would see him go past. When he did, I called to him. He asked what I wanted. I told him my mother's name and asked him if he remembered her. Certainly he did, he said; she was one of the unholy witches he burned in Bilstein. He mentioned a piece of the evidence he fabricated, about her having congress with the Devil on the eve of All Saints' Day and told me how she had enjoyed it. I told him she was my mother, at which he sneered that he pitied me, and I was fortunate to be an orphan if she was my last parent. And then he walked away laughing. I only wanted to make him understand what he was doing and stop his evil work.'

Theodemar's head drooped on his chest.

'I only wanted him to say he was sorry and would stop. That was all. But he would not. I grabbed the nearest thing without thinking what it was and chased after him. My habit hindered me but I caught him halfway along the corridor. He stumbled, fell to his knees, but somehow regained his feet and ran on. I hesitated but then chased after him, but my pause gave him enough time to gain the library and lock the door behind him. I waited for a few minutes in case he reappeared, but he did not, and I heard a thud as if he had collapsed. I was shocked to see that the object I had grabbed was the processional cross and that it was now bent, so I took it to my cell to clean and straighten, and then returned to mop the corridor. I could not sleep, but when I heard that his body had been found I knew that finally his wicked work would end.'

'But you could not straighten the cross?' I asked.

'Not without making a lot of noise. I cleaned it reverently and returned it to the treasury when Brother Ambrose opened it in the morning. I sneaked in behind his back.'

'And you were responsible for moving Armand's body.'

'I did not know if the old superstition was true. Some of them have a basis in fact, after all, even if we have forgotten what it was. I dragged it to the kitchen door and then used the cart to take it to the well.'

'I did not know there was a well,' I explained, 'but when the search was being organised and Father Prior was allocating areas I heard you volunteer to search the part of the grounds where the well proved to be. That's what made me think the body must be there — and gave me the idea that you must be the one who had reacted to what he said.'

Theodemar fell to his knees in front of the Prior. 'Father Prior, I submit to your judgement.'

The Prior looked nonplussed. What penance is suitable for a Brother who confesses to murdering a guest? 'Go to the chapel and pray for God's forgiveness while I take counsel of these wise men — and woman. Brother Andrew, Brother Nathaniel, go with him. And Brother Theodemar, know this. We will pray for the soul of your dear mother, not just today, but regularly.'

'Thank you, Father Prior. Thank you all. May God bless you.'

Theodemar was led out and the other brothers sent to their tasks.

'Well,' said the Prior, 'I would welcome advice on what I should do.'

Von Anethan was in no doubt. 'If we do not hand him to the authorities it will look as if the Church connives in a great sin.'

'On the other hand,' said Abbess Mathilde, 'what purpose is served by putting him to death? He will do no more great evil, and may yet do some good.'

I felt the same way, but held my peace.

'Armand has family,' Senguerdius reminded us. 'They are entitled to justice.'

The debate continued for some time. I just wanted to pack my bag and leave. There was nothing more for me to do here. I had found the criminal, and now I just wanted to get home to the clean air of Leiden and immerse myself in a book in the library.

It was, I think, Govarts who came up with the action the Prior finally took.

'I think, Father Prior, that you underestimate the esteem in which you are held by the citizens here. It is my belief that you could negotiate with the mayors that you will hand Theodemar over to the civic authorities for punishment on the understanding that they will not execute him.'

I heard some months later that Theodemar had been sentenced to perpetual confinement within the grounds of the church, allowed out only with the express permission of the Prior. How he was received by the other Brothers, I do not know. Nor do I know whether he ever found his sister, though Abbess Mathilde undertook to make enquiries of convents on his behalf and I am quite certain that if she could not find her, nobody could.

Those readers who have read my previous memoirs will know that I have accumulated some gold as reward for my work. I promised the Prior I would send a portion of it to the church to have the processional cross repaired. What better use could I make of it?

A couple of days later, late in the evening, our barge pulled alongside the fish market and Senguerdius and I climbed out and began walking to the Academy building.

'A great shame that we were deprived of our famous victory,' Senguerdius said. 'Van Espen's case was not strong. And I had some excellent arguments in our favour. Perhaps we should suggest a rematch next year rather than waste the research?'

I felt a shudder pass down my spine. 'Would it not seem as if we were taking advantage of the death of their key witness?' I suggested.

'You mean our win would be tarnished by the disadvantage Leuven faced?'

'Yes, Rector.'

He chewed this over for a few paces. 'You may be right, Mercurius. Best to put the whole thing behind us. We know we would have won, and that's what's important.'

I obediently kept my mouth shut.

'This inn you go to, Mercurius. Is it far?'

'It's on the way. Two minutes' walk from here.'

'Lead on, then. Let's have some noise and life after a time of peace and death.'

A NOTE TO THE READER

Dear Reader,

Thank you for picking up this book. Fifteen years have now elapsed between Mercurius' first adventure and this one, and a lot has happened in his life, but rest assured he still has more tales to tell. Whether Van der Meer can tolerate his master long enough to write them all down may be a different matter, though I am reassured that Van der Meer is mentioned in Mercurius' will, in terms of much greater affection than appears here.

I could hardly write about the seventeenth century and not mention witches, and I am indebted to Malcom Gaskill's book *Witchfinders* which relates events in the east of England but which gave me some ideas for this book. I also read *Malleus Maleficarum* and my opinion of it exactly coincides with that of Mercurius. I ought also to mention Professor Willem Otterspeer's magnificent history of the University of Leiden, *The Bastion of Liberty*. It could settle many arguments, especially if you hit someone with it. It's quite a weight.

Readers very kindly send me suggestions for topics, people and events that Mercurius may have encountered. Please keep them coming. They are always welcome. I hope this tale satisfies those who asked him to visit Maastricht and I am only sorry that I could not work André Rieu into the story somewhere.

I had to take some liberties with the history and geography of the Basilica of St Servatius. At the time of the story it had a garden around it and a small population of resident Brothers. Its treasury is now much expanded and well worth a visit, as is the city itself. There are few better places for sitting with a glass of wine or a *sjoef* and watching the world go by.

I must particularly thank friends in the Anglo-Netherlands Society who give me information that informs the books and spread the word about them. If you are in the UK and have an interest in Dutch life, take a look at www.anglo-netherlands.org.uk. You may find me at meetings.

I had the pleasure of revisiting Leiden while writing this book. It was a windy day and the fish market was in full swing, so it was relatively easy to imagine it as a busy place in the seventeenth century and picture the sights and sounds (and, in view of the fish, the smells).

If you have enjoyed this novel, I'd be really grateful if you would leave a review on **Amazon** and **Goodreads**. I love to hear from readers, so please keep in touch through **Facebook** or **Twitter**, or leave a message on my **website**.

Dank je wel!

Graham Brack

Sapere Books is an exciting new publisher of brilliant fiction and popular history.

To find out more about our latest releases and our monthly bargain books visit our website:
saperebooks.com

Printed in Great Britain
by Amazon

29587873R00123